FAIR CRONIES AND FELONIES

A RAINA SUN MYSTERY

ANNE R. TAN

FIRE IN THE HOLD

Raina Sun Louie glanced at the entrance to the game room and grimaced. *Here we go again*, she thought to herself. She ran a hand through her curly black hair, a recent tic she'd acquired to buy herself time to respond to the dueling duo.

Po Po stabbed a finger at her arch nemesis. Her grandma's pixie haircut had grown into a shag with long silver bangs that highlighted the anger in her brown eyes. Though barely over five feet tall, she was a force to be reckoned with.

Janice Tally, the social committee chair, batted at Po Po's finger with a knitting needle. Her grandma's arch nemesis was a bird of a woman with big round glasses and had recently taken to dying her hair black with a tint of blue like Marge from *The Simpsons*. She had no fear of rolling on toes with her walker and stabbing people's backside with her needles to prod them to do her bidding.

According to a Chinese proverb, the two of them must have mixed up their bones in a previous life. Sometimes her grandma took an opposing stance to get Janice riled up for entertainment. And Janice always took the bait. They just couldn't stay out of each other's business.

As the director for the senior center, Raina had to referee between these two strong-willed women daily. Her head pulsated with the beginnings of a headache. *Not today*, she thought. She turned, hoping to make a quick exit through the rear doorway that led to the communal kitchen before either of the ladies noticed her.

"Raina, great job at the town council meeting this morning," said an approaching familiar voice. "I'm sure your argument will make the council reconsider the budget cut for the center."

Raina glanced over her shoulder. Alonso Escalante rose from the game table. The other retirees were packing up the Scrabble game and leaving the room. Probably to get ready for the potluck later in the evening or to get away from the dueling duo. No one wanted to pick sides.

She glanced at the doorway again. Luckily, Po Po and Janice were still there, having their showdown. Raina couldn't hightail it out of the room with the center's biggest financial donor wanting a chat. "I'm just doing my job."

"I can always tell when someone does a job from the heart. To some people, us old folks are nothing but a burden," Alonso said, placing a hand over his heart. "But you, my dear, actually care about us."

Raina blushed. It really wasn't much. She already spent time at the senior center because of her grandma, only now she was getting paid to help organize things. "Thank you. I appreciate the kind words." She had learned a long time ago never to dismiss a compliment.

"If the Council ends up cutting the budget, I can make a bigger donation this year to make up the shortfall," Alonso said.

Originally from Spain, Alonso still had a Spanish accent even though he had lived in the United States for more than fifty years. His olive skin was rough as jerky, but instead of caramelizing into a beautiful tan color, it was blotchy with age spots that fell into crevices created by his deep wrinkles. But what he lacked in the physical appearance department, he made up for with his generous heart.

Raina hesitated. She appreciated his offer. However, once the budget was cut, the senior center would not get the funds back without a fight. And private donations were not a guaranteed annual funding source.

"Rainy!" Po Po called from the entrance. In

Chinese, Po Po was the formal title for a maternal grandmother and also a term of respect for elderly ladies. Her legal name was Bonnie Wong.

Raina met Alonso's eyes and groaned involuntarily.

Alonso chuckled. His hazel eyes sparkled with amusement. "That's my cue to pick up the smoked brisket from my cook. I'll see you at the potluck later."

As he stepped around Raina, his cell phone rang. He answered it and stepped through the rear doorway to the communal kitchen of the senior center. From there, he could circle around back to the foyer or leave the building through the side exit. The lucky man.

Resigned, Raina turned to face the music. If only it weren't a Chinese opera full of waving hands, stomping feet, and echoing voices. And in the end, someone would be reduced to tears—hopefully, they wouldn't be hers.

Po Po and Janice scowled at each other, their eyes narrowing, neither daring to break eye contact.

Raina shifted her weight to the other foot. Maybe she could make a run for the kitchen before either woman noticed her disappearance.

As if Raina's movement was a signal, both women flew into a flurry of activity.

Janice Tally pushed her walker to the left, reducing the gap between the wingback reading chair and the table. She jabbed at the air with her knitting needle while shuffling forward with the walker one-handed.

Po Po swerved around her arch nemesis and bolted

for the gap between the board game table and the ping-pong table. Unencumbered by a medical device, she made better time even though she took the more circuitous route.

Janice abandoned the walker and threw the knitting needle at Po Po, who ducked, shook a fist, and called out a mean name. Janice made a beeline for Raina, ignoring the name-calling.

Raina's eyes widened. Her grandma had been right all along. The walker had been a ploy to gain sympathy. Should she laugh or tell the ladies to slow down? What if one of them broke a hip?

Though they were moving at top speeds for their age, to Raina, they appeared as if they were moving underwater. She settled on a neutral expression, though she was sure her dark brown eyes were twinkling with amusement.

Po Po skidded to a stop in front of Raina, her orthopedic shoes squeaking on the wood floor. "You asked me to post signs in the kitchen, so I did. Now Janice is complaining about the signs."

Raina groaned inwardly. It had sounded like a simple job for her grandma to post fliers around the kitchen this morning. The emergency water main repair in the street had shut down the fire suppression system in the building. The facility person was supposed to return in an hour to turn the system back on. All the retirees who signed up for the potluck were notified of this inconvenience and were told to heat their food at home. It should have been a brainless job. How did it lead to World War III between these two ladies?

She raked at her curly black hair again. It probably stood out around her head even more from the attention. A Chinese girl with an Afro wasn't someone who could handle these two Titans. What was she thinking when she took the job? Would the town fire her if she couldn't handle these two?

Janice shuffled over the last few steps and took several deep breaths, her hands over her heart.

Po Po opened her mouth to steamroll over Janice, but Raina held up her hand. "Please let Janice catch her breath, so she can have her say."

Her grandma crossed her arms and harrumphed. She had no patience for the social committee chair who had banned her from all the major events in the last year.

This rivalry between the two ladies was the hardest part of Raina's new job. She could handle budget cuts, but she wasn't sure how to navigate this rivalry without hurting someone's feelings, especially with a grandma who expected family loyalty to come first.

The corners of Janice's lips twitched, and she slowed her breathing even more, taking her sweet time and knowing it would irritate Po Po.

"Bonnie plastered the entire kitchen with her fliers," Janice said. "It looks ridiculous. Who tapes paper on top of the electrical burners on the stovetop? It's a fire hazard."

"The whole point is to make somebody stop and think before using the stove," Po Po said. "If someone sees a sheet of paper on top of the burner, who would be stupid enough to turn it on?"

Raina held up the universal time out sign, forming a "T" with her hands. "Whoa! Why don't we go take a look in the kitchen?"

The two ladies opened their mouths—

An alarm began to wail from a distance, and the smoke detectors in the game room picked up its tune.

Raina's eyes widened, finally noticing the smoke coming in from the rear doorway. Her heart began to beat faster, matching a rising fear. This was no fire drill. Someone must have used the kitchen and started a fire. *Please don't let Po Po have anything to do with this,* she pleaded silently to her ancestors.

THICK TENDRILS of smoke billowed out of the kitchen, and the heat blasted across Raina's face. She squinted at the dim interior. "Anyone in here? Alonso, are you in here?" she screamed from the doorway.

While she had seen Alonso disappear into the kitchen a few minutes ago, he had no reason to still be in there. With three exits to choose from, he must have left the building before the fire started. And yet, until

Raina got confirmation that he was safe, she worried about him.

Manny Díaz, a warden for the fire evacuation team, ushered several senior citizens toward the exit of the center. His silver hair and orange construction vest were beacons in the darkening interior. His walkie talkie blared as he communicated with the evaluation teams. He came back and grabbed Raina's arm.

"We need to get out of here," Manny said, coughing at the smoke. "Janice and Bonnie are doing the roll call outside. They'll let us know if someone is missing."

Raina nodded and squinted at the smoke and dancing flames in the kitchen one more time. "Anyone in here?" She waited, straining her eyes and ignoring the tickling in the back of her throat. If she gave in to it, she would probably start coughing too.

The fire crackled and roared, leaping into the air. No answer. Whoever started the fire probably ran off, afraid of being caught. Was this an accident or arson?

Raina reluctantly left with Manny. She hoped the quarterly fire drills were enough to get everyone safely outside. Janice Tally, Po Po, and another retiree were checking folks off in the corner of the parking lot.

The maintenance crew working on the water main were in the process of covering up the trench on the ground with metal plates. Attached to the excavator bucket was a chain with a heavy duty magnet, dangling a metal plate above the open trench. The heavy equipment operator and the rest of the crew gaped at the commotion.

Raina ran across the parking lot, waving her hands in the air like a crazy woman. "There's a fire in the building. The fire truck is coming!"

The wail of emergency vehicles approached them. As the sounds came closer, the maintenance workers swiveled their heads back to the street as if looking for the source of the sirens.

"Cover up the street! The fire truck is coming!" Raina yelled from sidewalk.

A man leapt out of a parked truck and yelled at the maintenance crew. "Quick! Cover up the street!" He must be the foreman.

The heavy equipment operator lowered the excavator bucket with the metal plate and a worker attached a metal stick to guide the plate over the open trench. Once in place, the worker signaled for the operator. The plate dropped with a loud bang. The worker removed the guiding stick, and the foreman detached the chain.

Several blocks away, a fire truck turned the corner, its lights flashing and sirens blaring. It raced toward the senior center.

A walkie-talkie crackled to life. "It won't stop in time!"

It was the flagger screaming into the walkie-talkie. He was a block away, holding the "STOP" sign with shaking hands. His orange vest was not much protection against several tons of steel barreling toward him.

The heavy equipment operator, sweat pouring down his face and dampening his shirt, moved the tractor to the side of the road. It was still blocking a third of the lane. As the machine came to a stop, the operator jumped out.

At the first orange construction sign on the road, the fire truck slammed on the brakes. The flagger tossed the "STOP" sign and leapt out the way. The maintenance crew ran for the parking lot. Raina took several steps back, her heart racing with adrenaline.

The fire truck slowed and made a wide arc around the tractor and into the parking lot, rattling the metal plates on the road. It pulled up next to the building, and the fire crew jumped out of the vehicles. Like a well-practiced orchestra, every person knew their task and performed it on reflex.

The foreman swore and glanced at Raina sheepishly.

The metal plate rattled again, and she glanced up to see a police cruiser with an ambulance at its bumper pulling into the parking lot. The emergency medical technicians grabbed their medical bags and headed toward the group of retirees.

Raina scanned the crowd, found Po Po and Janice, and joined them. "Everyone accounted for?"

"Alonso didn't sign out of the visitors log," Janice said with a worried expression.

"People don't always sign in or out," Po Po said, putting a cheerful spin on the situation. "Without someone monitoring all the exits, there's no way to know who is coming and going."

Raina frowned. She prayed this was the case, and Alonso was safely in his mansion worrying about transporting his smoked brisket.

A fireman came out of the building and jogged over to join them.

Raina recognized the fire chief and stepped forward to greet him. "Everyone is accounted for, except Alonso Escalante. I saw him go into the kitchen before the fire, and he said he was heading home. But he didn't sign out on the visitors log, so we don't know if he had actually left the building."

The fire chief nodded and pressed a button near his shoulder, which probably activated the two-way radio. He spoke into it, relaying Raina's information about Alonso.

As the fire chief jogged back to join his crew, he called over his shoulder, "Raina, make sure everyone stays here until you get the all clear."

Officer Youri Sokol got out of the police cruiser and exchanged a few words with the fire chief. He glanced at the group of retirees and frowned like he was studying a bunch of arsonists. It was precisely this attitude and his haphazard investigations that led to his demotion from detective to officer. It had been several months, but he still walked around with a boulder on his shoulder.

He sauntered over to Raina. He was a doppelgänger for Danny DeVito, but his pug face was often set in a scowl. He was just as height challenged as Raina, approximately two or three inches taller. But this didn't stop him from looking down at her, which meant he held his nose up like he had a nose bleed.

"Why am I not surprised to see you here?" he said.

Raina bit back a smart comment. There was no point in riling the man up when he clearly didn't want to be here. "Do you need anything from me? Are you taking a police report?"

Officer Sokol narrowed his eyes at Raina. "Is there a crime here?"

Raina shrugged. "I don't know. I'm hoping it's all an accident."

"Then I guess I'm not needed," he said and got back into his police cruiser.

As Raina watched the disgruntled officer drive away, she wondered why he came out in the first place if he didn't intend to help.

Two hours later, Raina got the all clear that the fire was put out, and the senior citizens could return to their condos. Many of them were sitting on the asphalt and leaning against each other. It looked like the potluck was a complete bust.

The fire chief pulled Raina aside and whispered,

"We found a body in the kitchen. The police are on the way."

Raina swallowed the bile rising in her throat. "Is it Alonso Escalante?"

The fire chief nodded. "That's the name on his driver's license. I'm sorry."

A wave of guilt washed over Raina. "I didn't hear anyone in the kitchen. With the smoke, I couldn't see inside. I should have run inside the kitchen. I might have been able to save Alonso."

The fire chief patted Raina's shoulder. "Don't be too hard on yourself. You would have run into trouble trying to get him out by yourself. You're not strong enough to drag out a man his size."

"Drag out? He didn't...uh...burn?"

"No, the fire didn't touch him. He might have died from the smoke inhalation. The coroner will be able to confirm how Alonso died."

Despite what the fire chief said, Raina couldn't help but wonder if she had failed Alonso somehow. She didn't think he would still be in the kitchen. If he wasn't burned, then he wasn't close to the flames. Then why didn't he leave through the side exit? Unbidden, an even more morbid thought drifted through her mind. What if he was prevented from leaving the kitchen?

2

MISBEHAVING

Later that evening, Raina and Po Po had homemade pizza and a side salad for dinner in Raina's dining room. Luckily, she always kept a frozen pizza crust in the freezer for Matthew. For toppings she brushed on olive oil, a sliced bell pepper, ham, and cheese. It wasn't fancy, but it was lower sodium than take-out, which would keep her grandma's ankles from swelling the next morning.

They could have the Oreo cookie cheesecake she'd made for the potluck later. With the potluck cancellation, she hoped the senior citizens had food at home, especially those who signed up to bring napkins, plates, and cutlery.

The forensic team, police, and fire chief were still at the senior center finishing up their work at the crime scene. Raina had left the spare key with Detective Joanna Hopper, the lead detective. When Raina dropped Po Po off at her condo later, she could check to make sure the doors of the senior center were locked up for the night. There wasn't anything worth stealing at the center, but vandalism repair wasn't something she wanted to add to her long to-do list and anemic budget.

Raina and Po Po wolfed down their food. After the discovery of the body, it had taken the police another hour after their arrival to dismiss the senior citizens. Raina had pulled Detective Hopper aside and convinced her to let the retirees go by promising to give her a list of names and phone numbers tomorrow. If Raina hadn't done this, who knew how much longer they would have to wait in the parking lot.

Po Po put a bite of cheesecake in her mouth and sighed with contentment. "I feel so much better now. I was getting hangry from all the waiting around."

Hangry was slang for cranky from hunger. When Po Po got hangry, there was no telling what would come out of her mouth.

"Good thing you're happy now," Raina said. With the warm fuzzies that came from a full stomach, the tensions of the day drained away.

Po Po took a sip of water. "What do you think happened to Alonso? What was he doing in the kitchen? The man can't even scramble eggs for breakfast."

"He got a phone call right before you and Janice..." Raina's voice trailed off, and she hesitated. She didn't want to use the words "ambushed me," even though it was exactly how she felt. "Came to me with your little disagreement."

Po Po smirked. "Just call me out. I know I misbehaved."

Raina's lips twitched, and she suppressed the urge to laugh. "I'm glad you're aware of your behavior. Why do you do it?"

"Because I'm old and I can. It's the highlight of my day," Po Po said matter-of-factly.

The two of them laughed out loud.

Po Po's logic made perfect sense to Raina, but it still didn't make her job any easier. It was probably time to play her trump card. "I don't mind you having fun with your arch nemesis, but can't you keep me out of it? It makes my job so much more difficult. I might have to quit."

Po Po's eyes widened. "You can't quit. I need you on my side."

"Exactly this! I can't play favorites," Raina said, giving her grandma a pointed look. "How will it look to the rest of the members?"

Po Po harrumphed and crossed her arms. "Fine. Play by the book. I'd rather win some and lose some, than to not win at all."

Raina gave her grandma a cheeky grin. "In other words, you want me to call you out when you're misbehaving."

"Just not too loud. I don't want Smelly Tally to make me eat crow."

"Could you please stop calling her Smelly Tally? Someday the nickname will come out of my mouth. I would die of embarrassment," Raina said.

"But she does smell like a little old lady with her mothballs and rose-scented paper. It reminds me of my grandma," Po Po said.

Raina sighed. Po Po was incurable. Janice was only two years older than her grandma. "Just try, okay? Do it for me."

Po Po sighed. "Only for you."

"Back to the fire," Raina said. "It was an unfortunate accident, and now we can't use the kitchen for weeks. Insurance will not pay for all the food in the refrigerators for the hot meal program."

"What about take-out?"

"That can get pricey," Raina said, chewing her lower lip. "Maybe Brenda Sullivan can give us a deal."

If Raina called in the food orders to the Venus Café this evening, Brenda might be able to shop, cook, and pack the lunches for the meal program. But the timing would be tight. And the expense would hurt the center's even tighter budget.

"After what you've done for her family, she owes you," Po Po said.

Raina covered her face with her hands. What a disaster, especially since she hadn't even passed probation yet. She would be lucky if the Town Council didn't fire her on the spot.

"How do you know the fire wasn't arson?" Po Po asked.

Raina glanced up in surprise. "Arson? Why would somebody want to burn down the senior center?"

"Someone could have set the kitchen on fire to hide the evidence. Or to confuse the issue?"

"Evidence for what?"

"Alonso's murder."

Raina gaped at her grandma. Trust Miss Marple on training wheels to jump head first into an investigation without all the facts. "Who would want to kill Alonso? He was such a nice guy."

"His former business partner and his ex-wife," Po Po said, ticking the points off on her fingers. "There might be others lurking in the background. You don't become a multi-millionaire without stepping on some toes."

"Who is his former business partner?" Raina asked.

"Manny Díaz. He hates Alonso's guts. Manny always felt that Alonso kicked him to the curb, causing him to miss out on the millions that Alonso made after the partnership dissolved. He tells everyone who will listen to this story."

"The Manny who is the fire warden for the senior center?"

"That's him," Po Po said. "And now, in his retirement, he does handyman stuff to help with the finances."

Raina sat back in her chair and frowned. Now this was a complication she hadn't considered. She already had her hands full with the budget, probably multiple memos to the City Council, and an insurance claim to file. Not to mention her other part-time job at the Venus Café. "Manny hasn't told me this story."

"Give it some time. He'll get to it. If there's something suspicious about Alonso's death, we need to investigate it," Po Po said.

Raina shook her head. "I already have too much on my plate. If—and that's a big if—there is a murder investigation, that is Detective Hopper's job."

"Matthew is out of town. Joanna Hopper is still green as a newly minted detective. And the former Detective Sokol probably wants to get Joanna back for replacing him. They will make a mess of this case without our help."

Raina sighed and reached for her glass of water. She hated it when her grandma was right. "We'll cross that bridge when we get there. No need to borrow any more trouble tonight."

The next morning, Raina stood at the entrance of the kitchen, staring with dismay at the damage inside. The walls and ceiling were black. The stovetop that was the source of the fire was partially melted, along with the wood counter next to it. On the ground, by the damaged stovetop, was the chalk outline of the body.

She didn't dare to step inside and cross the crime scene tape. Why didn't Alonso go home? Did the phone call change his mind?

The communal kitchen lay between the game room and the recreation room, the all-purpose room that reminded Raina of a high school gymnasium without the basketball courts and the bleachers. She stepped inside the game room and groaned. While there was no fire damage inside, some of the smoke had crept onto the wall of the rear exit that connected the room to the kitchen. She couldn't let the senior citizens hang out in this room until the smoke damages were repaired. She took a deep breath. Yuck! The room would have to be aired out as well.

Next, she went to check on the recreation room, usually just called the rec room. Like the game room, there was smoke damage on the wall that connected the room to the kitchen. Luckily, the rec room was large enough that she could still have the hot meal for the seniors in the opposite end of the room. With Brenda Sullivan willing to supply take-out meals from the Venus Café, Raina should be able to keep the hot meal program running.

Raina posted signs up on the game room doorway to let the retirees know the room was closed until further notice. She figured they would know the kitchen was off limits from the crime scene tape. Then she went into her shoebox of an office to call the insurance company and write a memo to the Town Council about the fire.

Throughout the morning, several senior citizens drifted downstairs from the condo complex to check on their beloved center. Raina could hear them through her closed office door, but luckily, none of them knocked. Much as she would like to start questioning folks about the fire, she had to take care of business first.

A couple hours later, she used the bathroom and checked the setup in the rec room. The five college students that helped with the hot meal program usually prepared the meals for school credit and a small stipend from the center. Raina had sent them an email last night explaining the situation and asked them to set up the tables and chairs when they came in for their shift. Not only had they finished the setup, but they also arranged a check-in table for the seniors to sign for their meals.

"Can someone help me with the food? It's outside in the van," Raina said.

All the students went outside with Raina. The Venus Café catering van was parked next to the curb. Brenda was loading a cart with take-out bags. She handed each of them a tray full of take-out bags. When the senior citizens drifted in for their meals, Raina left the meal distribution and cleanup to the students. She grabbed a take-out bag and the iced coffee with her name on it.

For the first time all morning, Raina could finally breathe. She locked her office door and went out to the garden to enjoy her lunch in peace. While biting into her sandwich, a shadow fell across her face. She glanced up, blinking.

"I found you at last," Detective Joanna Hopper said. "What are you doing, hiding out here by yourself?" She was a willowy blonde with huge blue eyes and a cherubic face that reminded Raina of the fat babies in Renaissance paintings. She could have her pick of men, but for some reason, her relationships never worked out.

Raina slowly swallowed her bite of the hot pastrami sandwich and took a sip of iced coffee. "I had a busy morning. I needed time alone." She stressed the last word, hoping the detective would take the hint and leave.

"When is Matthew coming back from his vacation?" Detective Hopper asked, sitting down next to Raina on the wood bench.

"Two more weeks," Raina said, puzzled by the question.

The Gold Springs Police Department was small enough that everyone knew each other's schedules. A vacation of more than two days required shifting the workload around to stay on top of things. Why did Detective Hopper ask such a rhetorical question?

"What is he doing in China anyway?" Detective Hopper asked.

"He's there for the Ching Ming Festival." At Detective Hopper's frown, Raina continued, "It's when Chinese families sweep the ancestral burial ground to get rid of cobwebs and bugs. They don't have groundskeepers in old villages like we do here at the cemeteries. We bring food, wine, joss paper, and incense to make offerings to our ancestors and ask for their blessing. Mostly it's a family get-together at the graveyard. When you bring all that food, you have to eat it afterwards."

Detective Hopper nodded. "Kind of like the Day of the Dead."

"But without the music, the colors, and the face painting," Raina said. Compared to the Mexican tradition, Ching Ming sounded rather dull. Traditional Chinese culture prized obedience and honor rather than embracing a vibrant life.

"So why aren't you in China?"

Raina grimaced. If she had gone to China, she could have pretended it was her honeymoon. "New job. Not enough vacation days yet."

"The whole Louie family went? Including Matthew's estranged father?"

"Yes, Matthew's father and his grandma went with him. His brother stayed behind. I don't think Blue is ready for China," Raina said. Matthew's half-brother was half Chinese and was raised by his Italian mother.

Detective Hopper shifted uncomfortably, twirling her blonde braid around her fingers.

Raina ignored the policewoman and returned to her sandwich. Detective Joanna Hopper wanted something from Raina. All those questions about Matthew were just awkward small talk. Raina was curious, but she wasn't willing to make it easy on the detective.

When they first met, Joanna Hopper took an instant dislike to Raina. It was a one-sided romantic rivalry over Matthew that fizzled out because Raina never engaged, and Matthew never even noticed Joanna's interest. Over the years, the dislike turned into a grudging respect as Raina solved several murder investigations. And recently, they had formed a tenuous friendship over their mutual dislike of Officer Sokol. But this friendship could just as easily dissolve into thin air.

Detective Hopper cleared her throat. "Alonso Escalante didn't die from smoke inhalation. He was hit with a blunt object that caused a severe skull fracture. He died from the brain injury."

3

AN OLD ALLY

Raina's eyes widened, and she hastily swallowed her bile. Just as her grandma suspected, someone had set the kitchen on fire to hide the murder. Her pulse jumped at the disturbing thought. *Poor Alonso*, she thought. She hoped he didn't suffer before his death. "Why are you telling me this?"

Detective Hopper watched Raina closely as if waiting for a reaction. "I thought you might like to know. Seeing as how Alonso is the biggest private donor for the center."

Raina felt numb. Who would hurt a kind man like Alonso on purpose? "There must be a mistake. Maybe he slipped and fell. Elderly people fall all the time." Even as she uttered the words, it rang false in her ears.

"Did Alonso have trouble getting around? Did he need a cane or a walker?"

Raina shook her head. "Quite the opposite. He attended the senior exercise classes just as religiously as my grandma."

"Was the kitchen floor wet or newly waxed?"

Raina shook her head again. As she finally accepted the truth, her heart sank. Somebody had murdered the poor man. A man she had considered a supporter and friend.

"Someone killed Alonso and set the kitchen on fire," she finally said. "How did this person know the fire suppression system was offline? We only found out about the water main leak yesterday morning. That's why it's called an emergency repair."

Detective Hopper folded her arms across her chest and waited.

Raina's mind whirled. The murderer had to be an insider at the senior center. It was a crime of opportunity. "You suspect someone at the senior center?"

Detective Hopper nodded.

Raina's thoughts drifted to what her grandma had said about Manny Díaz, the former business partner. "Even if this were true, what do you want from me?"

Detective Hopper gave her a long-suffering look. "Since it's an insider job, I would need an insider to help me crack the case. This person would be you. You can be my Watson."

Raina didn't need accolades, but she wasn't playing second fiddle again. She had played this role for Officer Sokol on many occasions, and looked at where that had landed her—on his naughty list. That man would take any opportunity to make life uncomfortable for her. She wasn't making that mistake again, no matter how much she liked Detective Hopper.

"I don't have time, Joanna," Raina said. "I have to deal with the insurance and get contractors to come out and make the kitchen's repairs. I still have to handle the Town Council and the budget cut. On top of this, I still have my part-time job at the Venus Café."

"You can be my eyes and ears at the café, too. All the gossip in town eventually makes its way there," Detective Hopper said, smiling at the thought.

"Matthew has never asked me to help with his investigations. I'm not even an amateur. Just a nosy busybody," Raina said slowly, hoping to discourage this bizarre conversation. Normally the police told her to butt out of their cases.

Detective Hopper's baby blue eyes pleaded with Raina. "I would not ask for your help if Matthew were here to help me. This is my first case as a lead detective. I can't mess this one up. The only help I've got is Youri Sokol, and he is still mad that I'm his replacement for this position. Do you think he's going to help me?"

Raina sighed in resignation. If she said no, it would probably damage their budding friendship beyond repair. She would like to keep their friendship so that she didn't have another enemy at the police station.

And Detective Hopper had her hands tied with

Officer Sokol. She would be lucky if he just ignored his duties. More likely than not, he would probably sabotage this case to get his revenge.

But most important of all, Alonso deserved justice. And he shouldn't have to wait until the police department straightened out their personnel issues to get it.

Raina sighed. Duty was heavier than a mountain. "All I am promising is to keep my eyes and ears open. The rest is up to you."

Detective Hopper gave Raina a beaming smile. "I knew I could count on you."

Raina suppressed the urge to groan out loud. It sounded like the detective's expectations were more than conveying gossip and hearsay. "Can you tell me anything else about the crime scene? What started the fire?"

"I haven't gotten the report from the fire department yet. You'll get a copy for the insurance," Detective Hopper said.

"Alonso got a phone call right before he left the game room. Can you pull his phone records to see who called him?" Raina asked. Even as the words left her mouth, she wondered if her grandma's hacker would be able to obtain this information faster than the police.

Detective Hopper's eyes widened. "Do you think someone lured him into the kitchen?"

"Your guess is as good as mine. It might be something, or it might be nothing."

"Were you the last person to interact with Alonso before his death?"

Raina shrugged. "I don't know."

"Who else was in the game room at the time?"

Raina rattled off a list of names, including Po Po and Janice Tally.

Detective Hopper wrote them down in her notebook. "Do you remember seeing anyone lurking about in the kitchen?"

Raina gave herself a mental head slap. She had to remind herself that the detective had to ask these kinds of questions to get to the truth. It just seemed silly after their earlier conversation. If Raina had noticed the murderer twirling his little mustache inside the kitchen, she would have said so already.

"I wasn't in the kitchen, so I don't know," Raina said.

The detective ran through a list of questions, and Raina tried her best to answer them without showing her impatience.

Finally, Detective Hopper closed her notebook and said, "Thanks for your time, Raina. I hope the next time we talk, you'll have more information for me. Do you have that list of people who were at the center yesterday?"

Raina pulled out a crumpled sheet from her purse. "I wrote down all the names I could remember and their phone numbers. Can I have the spare key back?"

She didn't want the police to have access to the center any time they wanted.

Detective Hopper's eyes shifted like she was considering not returning the key. There was an awkward moment where she dug around in her pockets before finally producing the key. She handed it over to Raina. "The forensic team will be coming back this afternoon to work on the crime scene."

Raina nodded. "When will they get done? I need to get estimates on the repairs. The contractors will need to get inside the kitchen. And I want to get rid of the chalk outline of the body."

"We will be out of your hair after today."

"Can I tell the retirees who died? Or is that still hush-hush? I would like to send a newsletter out about the fire."

"Give me until this afternoon."

As Raina watched Detective Hopper strolled back into the senior center, probably to interview other people, she wondered if she had made a mistake. While Alonso deserved justice, was teaming up with a newly minted detective the way to go about it? She knew what it felt like—this urge to prove herself at a new job—but her job wasn't a life or death situation. Would wanting to prove herself blind Detective Hopper to finding the real murderer?

AFTER LUNCH, Raina looked through her stash of cards and selected a few sympathy cards. She would lay it out on the narrow table at the foyer later this afternoon. She whipped out her cell phone and texted her grandma.

I NEED TO TALK TO MANNY DÍAZ.

Raina's cellphone chirped with a reply back from Po Po.

I'M IN HIS LIVING ROOM RIGHT NOW. UNIT 225. COME UP HERE.

Raina blinked at the message, reading it again to make sure she got it right. Was Po Po investigating Alonso's murder without her? She randomly grabbed a sympathy card from the table and trotted through the set of double steel doors that connected the foyer of the senior center to the lobby of the senior condo complex. During business hours, these doors were unlocked, allowing the senior citizens to go from their homes directly to the center conveniently.

As Raina waited for the elevator, she glanced around the lobby. The automatic double steel doors were supposed to close off the residential side of the building during a fire. There was no damage to the lobby. Thank goodness no one else was hurt from the incident yesterday.

Her hand curled into a fist, and she suppressed a sudden flash of anger. She couldn't believe the murderer would callously risk the lives of the senior citizens at the facility. No wonder her grandma didn't wait for Raina to start the investigation. If what Detective Hopper suspected were true, then there was a murderer among the retirees.

Raina jogged to Manny Díaz's unit, running through a list of scenarios in her head. The sympathy card was a decoy to get Alonso's former business partner to talk. She knocked on the door.

"It's unlocked. Come on in," called out a gruff man's voice.

Raina opened the door a crack and peered in as if expecting an ambush. With her grandmother, sometimes she didn't know what to expect. Po Po and a Hispanic elderly gentleman were having iced lemonades. She opened the door wider and stepped through, closing it behind her.

The home was a standard one-bedroom condo. The furniture would be characterized as shabby chic, secondhand stuff from the flea market. The blinds were closed, but sunlight filtered in between the cracks and the broken slats. A fan spun lazily on the ceiling, stirring up dust and stale air.

Manny Díaz was tall and thin, reminding Raina of a walking stick. He was of the same coloring as an insect, a dark olive complexion and deep brown eyes. His hair was a dull white like dirty snow on the side of the road, but his smile was wide and was as false as the teeth in his mouth. He gestured for Raina to have a seat next to her grandma on the sofa.

When Raina sat down, dust rose from the seat cushion, and she held her breath to keep from coughing. "I hope I'm not interrupting."

"Oh, no. I was telling your grandma about my recent trip to Mexico," Manny said. "I spend a few months every year with my sister and her family. I own the house next door. They keep an eye on it for me," Manny said. "Do you want a glass of lemonade?"

Raina shook her head. "No, I'm okay. Thanks for getting everyone out of the building yesterday."

Manny waved aside her thanks. "Just doing my job." He leaned forward, his eyes gleaming. "I heard they found a body in the kitchen."

Raina gave her grandma a sharp look. What kind of rumors was her grandma spreading now?

Po Po held up both hands, palms out. "It wasn't me. I don't know how that got circulated."

"There is a chalk outline of a body on the ground," Manny said.

Raina rubbed her temples. There was no hiding the murder from the retirees. Either the retirees would hide in their homes, or they would form teams to see who could solve the case first. Great. "What else is circulating?"

"It's probably a murder," Manny said.

Raina cut another glance at her grandma.

"Will you stop looking at me, Rainy? I have nothing to do with this," Po Po said.

"It's the chalk outline and crime scene tape. We've seen enough television shows to know what that means," Manny said. "Do you know who died?"

Raina hesitated. The information would be common knowledge by this afternoon. And it would be helpful to see how Manny reacted to the death. "Alonso Escalante."

Manny turned ashen. When he reached for the lemonade, his hand shook. The liquid sloshed in the tall glass and spilled onto the carpet. He took a long sip like a drowning man. "*Dios Mio*," he muttered to himself.

Raina studied Manny. He didn't appear to be faking his shock. "Are you okay? I'm sorry. I didn't know you were close to Alonso."

"We weren't. Not close, that is," Manny said. He got up and went into the kitchen.

Raina glanced at Po Po, who shrugged.

Manny returned with a bottle of Oso Negro. He added a healthy splash of vodka to his lemonade and held out the bottle to Po Po. "Do you want some?"

Po Po shook her head and covered the top of her glass with her hand.

Manny set the bottle on the coffee table and took another swallow of his lemonade. "I can't believe this. Alonso was a pain, but who would kill him?"

Raina leaned forward in her seat. "I heard the two

of you had a falling out. Didn't you tell everyone he cheated you out of millions?"

"We had settled our differences," Manny said.

"What happened?" Raina asked. "Did Alonso apologize?"

"Alonso got the patent after I sold my half of the business to him. He didn't owe me anything." Manny took another swig of his lemonade.

Raina raised an eyebrow at her grandma but addressed Manny. "I find it strange that you have been bad-mouthing Alonso all these years, and suddenly you're upset at his death."

Manny narrowed his eyes at Raina. "What are you trying to say?"

Raina hesitated. Should she put the squeeze on Manny or pretend to be a concerned friend? "It doesn't look good for you, Manny. Alonso was an upstanding member of this community and generous to boot. He doesn't appear to have any enemies, except for you."

"I'm not his enemy."

"You say this now, but you told everyone for years that Alonso was a cheat ," Po Po said. "You told me the story a dozen times yourself."

Manny's jaw tightened. He took another sip of his lemonade. "What is this? Some kind of interrogation? You're not the police, and I don't have to tell you anything."

Raina shrugged nonchalantly. "Have it your way. The police will be here to talk to you soon enough."

And if information were a two-way street, she would probably get the gist of the police interview from Detective Hopper.

"Hold on," Manny said, licking his lower lip. "Why would the police want to talk to me?"

"What do you think, you big bimbo?" Po Po said. "You're a suspect. Probably on the top of their list."

If Manny was gray before, he turned white with fear. "No police. I don't want the police. You tell them that I had nothing to do with Alonso's death. Nothing."

"I can talk to the police for you, but they won't believe me," Raina said gently, hoping to calm Manny down. As if Detective Hopper would take Raina's word without interviewing the suspect herself. "They will want to know what happened between you and Alonso."

"You leave now," Manny said. His words were starting to slur, and he stumbled to the door. He held it open for them by leaning on it heavily.

Raina stood. The man was too gone with fear and alcohol to listen to sense. She would have to come back at another time.

Po Po followed Raina out. "We're leaving now." She said this louder than necessary.

Manny closed the door firmly behind them.

4

THE LION'S DEN

Po Po opened her mouth, but Raina shook her head. They probably shouldn't discuss the case right in front of the suspect's home. He could be on the other side, eavesdropping on them. They strode down the hall and got into the elevator.

"What were you doing alone in Manny's unit?" Raina said, not bothering to suppress the tension in her voice. "You knew he was a potential murder suspect."

Po Po waved away Raina's concern. "I'm wearing a wire. The Lovebirds are listening in across the hall in their unit. If they don't hear me leave, or if I scream, they will call the police."

Raina blinked. This explained why her grandma announced they were leaving in a loud voice. "By the time the police got here, you'd be dead. The Lovebirds are too weak to kick in Manny's front door."

Po Po pulled out a Taser from her pants pocket. "I have this. It should buy me some time."

Raina sighed. "Why didn't you wait for me?"

"I'm trying to save my breath to cool my porridge. There's no point in trying to convince you to do something you don't want to do. You're quite pigheaded."

Raina gave her grandma a deadpan expression. "Where do you think I get it from? The apple doesn't fall far from the tree."

Po Po's eyes twinkled, and she glanced at the elevator buttons. "Oh, geez. We forgot to hit the button."

Raina glanced at the panel and hit the button. Her mouth twitched. When she slid her gaze to her grandma, she burst out laughing. Po Po joined her half a second later.

As they stepped out of the elevator, Po Po said, "It looks like it's you and me again, Sherlock. With Matthew out of town, I don't think Detective Hopper will be able to accomplish much with Sokol shackled to her ankle."

Raina told her grandma about the conversation she had with Detective Hopper in the garden. "You're right on the money. She's afraid of sabotage as well. How can we get Manny to talk to us again?"

"I can always clog up my bathroom sink," Po Po said.

Raina studied her grandma for a long moment, not sure how to react. "Oookay," she said slowly. "Why?"

"Manny is a former plumber."

"I thought you said he's a handyman."

"He does a little bit of everything, but mostly plumbing. When Alonso bought out his share of the flooring business, Manny even tried to set up a rival business. But it went into bankruptcy. Then his wife died, and he spent some time in prison. When he came out again, he became a plumber. He takes care of everyone's plumbing in the building for cash. It's quite convenient to have him in the building."

Raina's jaw dropped. This was the reason her grandma made a good sidekick. She had gossip on everybody. "Is he just unlucky or what?"

"I think Manny is atoning for his previous life. But his son seems to walk in sunshine. Whatever he wants, he gets. He even got a free ride through medical school. Can you believe that?"

Raina wasn't sure if she believed in previous lives. For all she knew, this Chinese belief of karma and reincarnation might have been an ancient system created to keep people toeing the line. After all, if one was wicked, this person could—in theory—come back as a cockroach. And no one wanted to be a cockroach in their next life.

She nodded to acknowledge her grandma's comment. "The plan is to clog your sink and call Manny over to fix it. I can hide in your bedroom."

"I'll give Manny a call tomorrow. What's next?" Po Po asked.

"We'll drop off the sympathy cards and flowers tomorrow. We can have a chat with the housekeeper and Alonso's son. They both live at the mansion."

Po Po frowned. "Didn't Alonso have a daughter too?"

Raina nodded. "He adopted his stepdaughter when he was married to his second wife. During their divorce, he got rid of the wife but somehow kept his stepdaughter. It was a strange arrangement."

"Do you think a family member killed Alonso?"

Raina shrugged. "Your guess is as good as mine. Unless we know what's in his will, we don't know who inherits the money. Unfortunately, there's a lot of money in this situation, which makes murder mighty tempting."

WHEN RAINA PULLED up to the circular driveway of Alonso's mansion the next day, she glanced around, expecting a chauffeur or valet to appear offering to park her old Honda Accord. The two-story Spanish hacienda had a row of arches on each floor with a walkway underneath that wrapped around the entire length of the mansion.

"Wow! How many people do you think live here?" Po Po asked. Her wide eyes scanned the structure. "This place is probably thirty thousand square foot. That's a lot of dusting. I would hate to be the maid."

Raina chuckled. Trust her grandma to notice the housework, especially since she rarely did it herself. "Alonso, his son, and the housekeeper, who also does the cooking. The adopted daughter has her own place. I'm assuming there must be other staff to maintain the house, but I don't think they live in, though."

"How do you know so much about the Escalantes?" Po Po's eyes twinkled.

Raina shrugged. "I listen to folks when they talk to me."

"Are you trying to get more money out of Alonso? If his family finds out about it, they won't be happy with you."

"It's the opposite. Alonso was trying to throw money at us. He even offered to make up the deficit if the City Council sticks to their budget cut." A wave of sadness swept over Raina, and she lost her smile. "He even hinted at establishing a non-profit to subsidize the activities fees for low-income senior citizens. He was such a good person."

Po Po squeezed Raina's hands. "We will get to the bottom of this. We can't let someone get away with his murder."

Raina hesitated at a traitorous thought. Once they started digging, they might find out about Alonso's secrets. Everyone had a side they didn't want others to know about. "What if we find out there was a dark side to Alonso? After all, someone wanted him dead. I'd rather hold on to the memories I have of him."

"When you live long enough, all of us have scars. You hope the good deeds outweigh the mistakes and poor judgments. Secrets generally don't hurt the dead. It's the living that wants to keep things buried," Po Po said.

Raina gave Po Po a sideways glance. Her grandma was one wise cookie. "Let's get this show on the road."

They strode up the tiled steps to the double front doors with stained glass cutouts. Raina rang the doorbell. They had sat in the car long enough that someone would have noticed their presence from inside the house. She shifted from foot to foot and glanced around the expansive lawn spotted with trees.

The potted flower arrangement in Raina's hands looked woefully inadequate under the circumstances. She knew Alonso had money, but seeing his mansion was something else entirely. She straightened. The retired folks at the senior center had cared enough to chip in for the arrangement. It was the thought that counted.

Raina rang the doorbell again. Odd. Someone should be home unless the staff decided to abandon a sinking ship. She pulled out her cell phone and called the mansion. It rang for several minutes, and someone finally picked up.

"Escalante residence," said a breathless woman's voice.

"Hi, this is Raina Sun from the senior center. I am

dropping off sympathy cards and flowers for the family," Raina said. "I am at your front door."

There was a long pause as if the person was digesting what Raina was saying. "Give me a minute. I'm on the second floor cleaning Mr. Gabriel's bathroom." She hung up without another word.

Raina put away her cell phone. "I think the housekeeper picked up and said she is on her way. I wonder if the doorbell is broken."

Po Po peered at the doorbell. "It's one of those smart doorbells where it can record you. You can access the video feed from an app. I highly doubt it is broken. People with money have staff to fix things."

Raina wondered why no one came to the door until she called. Did someone inside hope they would go away?

One of the front doors opened, and Linda William peered out at them. Raina had met the housekeeper during Alonso's New Year's Eve party.

Linda was in her late forties. She was about five foot eight with gray strands in her blonde curls. Instead of putting her long hair back into a bun or ponytail, she left it loose so that it hung like a lion's mane around her face. Her face was angular—ski slope nose, thin lips, and a sharp chin. Her body was lean and wiry with muscles that came from years of housework.

After a long silence, Linda finally asked reluctantly,

"How can I help you?" Her flinty gray eyes flickered from Raina to Po Po.

"Hi, Linda. I'm Raina Sun, a friend of Alonso's. I don't know if you remember me..."

Linda nodded. "I remember your hair. Not many Chinese girls with hair like yours."

Raina swallowed the urge to throw out a witty remark about Linda's wild mane. She gestured at her grandma. "This is Bonnie Wong, my grandma." She held out the potted flowers and sympathy cards. "And these are from Alonso's friends at the senior center. Alonso was a good man, and we will miss him."

The housekeeper stared at Raina for a long second, and her lower lip trembled. She took a deep breath. "Would you like to come into the kitchen for a cup of tea?"

The question caught Raina by surprise, but she nodded. Maybe the housekeeper wanted to talk to someone who cared about her boss. "I would love to have a cup of tea."

They walked through the foyer in silence. The house already felt like a mausoleum with their footsteps echoing on the colorful tile floor. The kitchen was at the rear of the house on the west wing.

As they stepped through the archway and into the kitchen, Raina's jaw dropped open. Commercial grade appliances, a large marble island, a walk-in pantry the size of a small room. There was even a full-size dining table with seating for eight in front of the windows that looked out into a Spanish courtyard with a water fountain. Raina could spend a lifetime having breakfast in this kitchen.

Linda pressed the lever on the electric kettle, and it started boiling immediately. She turned on the oven, pre-heated it, and pulled out cookie dough from the freezer. "Mr. Alonso had a sweet tooth, so I always have cookie dough ready. Do you want chocolate chip or oatmeal raisin?"

Raina glanced at her grandma, who shrugged as if to say it was Raina's call. "Chocolate chip sounds great." She set the potted plant and cards on the kitchen island.

The oven dinged, and Linda slid in a tray of cookies. She pulled out a teapot from a shelf and prepared the tea.

Raina wandered over to the window to look outside at the courtyard. "This view is amazing. This house is amazing. I am surprised Alonso spent as much time as he did at the senior center. I would never want to leave."

"I think Mr. Alonso got lonely. His children come and go as they please. This house is like a hotel for them," Linda said.

"Isn't the house a little big for the family?" Po Po asked.

"It was built when he was still married," Linda said. "I think Mr. Alonso had hoped to fill it with children and grandchildren. Multi-generation under one roof like in his home country. Unfortunately, he didn't end up with any grandchildren."

The oven dinged again, and Linda pulled out the tray of cookies. She used tongs to transfer them onto a plate on the tray with the teapot and mugs. She brought the tray over to the kitchen table.

Once they each had a steaming mug of tea in front of them and took a bite out of the warm cookies, Raina asked, "Is Gabriel home? I want to give him my condolences."

Linda's face twisted into a grimace. "He's out shopping for a new car." Her mouth tightened until her thin lips disappeared from view.

"You're kidding me?" Po Po said. "His father is not even in the grave yet."

Linda's eyes burned with fury. "The son is already spending his fortune. The ex-wife and former best friend showed up to inventory the items in the house. The only person who seems to be upset is the daughter. And Miss Flora is not even his biological daughter."

Raina blinked, digesting what Linda said. "Who is the former best friend?"

"Manny Díaz. I think he lives at the senior condo complex."

Raina nodded. "Yes, he does, but I thought Alonso and Manny ended the friendship years ago."

Linda shook her head. "Maybe Manny did, but not

Mr. Alonso. My boss still remembered Manny's birthday. He also sent cards at Christmas."

"Did they ever resume the friendship? I don't ever recall seeing the two of them together," Po Po said.

"I don't know, but Manny came by the house with Valerie Escalante yesterday. Miss Flora let them in," Linda said. Her tone implied that she would have barred the door.

"What were they doing at the house?" Raina asked.

"Looking at things, opening drawers, and making a list," Linda said.

"Did they come in the morning or afternoon?" Raina asked, wondering if Manny got in touch with Valerie before or after their interview with him at his condo.

"Sometime before dinner," Linda said.

Raina wondered if Manny was sober when he came through the house, not that it mattered. And why was Valerie with Manny? Were the two of them involved romantically?

"And what did you do?" Po Po asked and took a sip of tea.

"Nothing," Linda said. "What else can I do? Miss Flora let them in, and then she went into her room. I just followed them to make sure they didn't take anything. When I told Mr. Gabriel, he just shrugged and said he didn't care about the things in the house."

Raina glanced at her grandma. Yikes! The scavengers were already circling. "The items in the house belong to the estate. Alonso's lawyer would probably want to know about this."

Linda's eyes gleamed. "I can't call the lawyer."

"Why not?" Po Po asked.

"Because I'm the help," Linda said. "And if my new boss finds out about it, I might lose my job."

"So, you're staying on?" Raina asked.

"I would like to. I always thought I would stay with Mr. Alonso for another fifteen years and then retire. I mostly do the grocery shopping and prepare three meals. A maid service comes by to do the heavy cleaning, and I pick up in between. In exchange, I get room and board plus a salary. And Mr. Alonso was a darling man. So easy to look after." Linda's lower lip wobbled again. She took a deep breath to steady herself. "Mr. Gabriel might not want to keep the house. He thinks it's too big for a bachelor. I don't even know where to go. This house has been my home for the last fifteen years."

"On the day of the fire, Alonso said he was coming home to pick up the smoked brisket you prepared for him. Did he come home for it?" Raina asked.

Linda shook her head. "I waited and waited, but he never came by. I called to see if he wanted me to drop it off, but it went straight to voicemail."

"Were you here by yourself all day?" Raina asked.

"The gardener came and went," Linda said. "I was outside cooking the brisket on the grill. I packed the brisket up, so it could stay warm. He told me the water was turned off at the senior center, and the kitchen was off limits."

Raina wondered who else in the household knew the water was turned off at the senior center. His son and adopted daughter? "Did the police come by to talk to you?"

Linda nodded. "Detective Hopper said someone knocked out Mr. Alonso and left him to die in the kitchen." Her voice choked up at the end, and she jammed a cookie in her mouth to hide her expression.

Raina waited until Linda swallowed and asked, "Can you think of anyone who might want to harm Alonso?"

"No one. As I said, he was a darling man. He didn't have a mean bone in his body," Linda said.

Po Po twirled a hand in the air. "Who will inherit all this?"

Linda shrugged. "Probably his children. I don't know. You'll have to ask Ms. Goldberg."

"Does Alonso treat both his children the same? Flora is Valerie's daughter from a previous marriage, right?" Raina asked.

"Yes, but he adopted Miss Flora when she was a child," Linda said.

"But when Alonso and Valerie got divorced, did they share custody of Flora?" Raina asked.

"No. Alonso felt that Miss Flora should be with her mom. He didn't get in touch with Miss Flora again until she was an adult," Linda said. "But once they connected again, they were like peas in a pod. She came back to town to work her way up in the family business."

"Do you know why Alonso and Valerie got divorced?" Raina asked.

Linda shrugged. "I don't know. One day they were together, and the next day they were not. She moved out."

"How does the son feel about his long-lost stepsister?" Po Po asked.

Linda nibbled on her cookie with a thoughtful expression. "I don't think he cares one way or another. He knows he will get the bulk of the money because he's Mr. Alonso's biological son."

"Does Gabriel work at the family business too?" Raina asked.

"Mr. Gabriel is not a people person. His father gives him an allowance," Linda said.

Raina gave her grandma a sideways glance. For a self-made man, this kind of behavior seemed at odds with the Alonso she knew. Could this be a point of contention between father and son? Especially with Flora willing to work from the bottom up at the family business?

Linda glanced over Raina's shoulder and stiffened. Her thin lips clamped shut, and she rose from her chair on shaky legs.

Raina turned around slowly.

In the kitchen entryway stood a woman in her

sixties with caramel blonde hair that came from a discount store. Her face appeared to be permanently frozen by Botox, but her brown eyes glittered with anger. Her breasts were tussled up in a Wonderbra, creating a deep wrinkly cleavage that would have made Betty Boop envious. The woman wore a skin-tight leopard print top and skinny black jeans and heels.

With one hand on her hip, the woman said, "What is going on here? Your boss isn't in the grave yet, and you are already entertaining like this is your house?" Her voice dripped with ice.

5

———

BETTY BOOP

Raina rose from her seat and held out her hand. The woman was too old to be Flora, and Alonso had never mentioned a younger sister. "Hi, my name is Raina Sun. I am a friend of Alonso."

The woman stared at Raina's hand for a long moment. Even with her frozen Botox face, several thoughts flickered through her brown eyes. Finally, she held out a limp fish and touched Raina's fingers. She pulled her hand back quickly. "Valerie Escalante. Alonso's wife." Though her voice no longer dripped with ice, it held no warmth either.

Raina blinked at the woman's claim. "When did you and Alonso get remarried?"

Valerie straightened her shoulders and lifted her chin. "We never got divorced."

Raina's jaw dropped. Whenever Alonso had

referred to Valerie, he had called her the ex-wife. Something wasn't adding up here, especially since the housekeeper had thought the Escalantes were divorced as well.

"How come you're not in mourning clothes?" Raina asked.

Valerie shifted her gaze to Po Po's clothes, and the corners of her mouth twitched. "Black is not my color."

Po Po stepped up next to Raina. "I say you're trying to get in front of the line for Alonso's money. His son will probably have something to say about your claim."

Valerie's gaze shifted to Po Po. "And who are you?"

"Bonnie Wong. I was a close friend of Alonso from the senior center," Po Po said.

Valerie's gaze swept over Po Po from head to toe and back up again. "And what makes you an expert on my relationship with my husband?"

Raina cringed inwardly. The claim was too outrageous, so it had to be true. But even if the Escalantes were still technically married, they had not lived together for more than a decade. For all Valerie knew, Alonso could have a special lady friend.

Po Po held up both hands, palms facing Valerie. "I'm not here to get into an argument with you. We're here to express our condolences. And if you are still married to Alonso, you need a lawyer."

The corners of Valerie's eyes tightened, but the rest of her face was still a blank slate. "Why would I need a lawyer?"

"For when you're charged with Alonso's murder. After all, the wife is always the prime suspect," Po Po said.

Valerie blinked and burst out laughing until tears ran down the corners of her eyes. Linda sank into her seat at the table. Raina and Po Po shared a confused look.

"There's a prenuptial agreement. Alonso is worth more to me alive than dead," Valerie finally said. "Upon his death, I only get a small settlement."

"What about your daughter? Alonso adopted her. Maybe you killed Alonso so your daughter could get a big inheritance," Po Po said. "Maybe she is willing to share with Mommy."

Raina gave her grandma a sideways glance. Usually, Po Po was much more subtle with her questioning. Something about Valerie must have gotten under her skin.

"You're out of line here. You're lucky I don't have a manservant to throw you out. Now get out before I call the police," Valerie said. She swung her gaze to Linda. "One more infraction like this, and you're out on the street."

Linda cowered at the table and began to clean up the tea and cookies. She averted her gaze when she shuffled past Raina to the kitchen sink.

Raina folded her arms across her chest. She hated when people throw their weight around, especially around those less fortunate than them. "I call your bluff. Please call the police. I know Alonso, and he had no reason to lie about his divorce. You might have kept his last name, but I bet your name is not even on the deed. How did you get in here? Do you have your daughter's keys?"

Valerie's gaze shifted and lost some of its fire. "I don't have time for this. Linda, see these people out." She turned around and sauntered to another part of the mansion.

Linda showed them out but didn't make any further conversation. She silently closed the door behind them.

RAINA PULLED AWAY from the circular driveway and followed the path to the road. Once the mansion was out of sight, she breathed a sigh of relief. "Valerie is something."

"Yeah, she's a pile of smelly poo," Po Po said.

"Do you think Alonso was still married to Valerie?" Raina asked.

Po Po shrugged. "You can check the court records. A divorce decree is public information."

Raina noticed her grandma didn't volunteer to do the records checking. It was beneath her pay grade to do tedious work. "It is a second marriage, so there had to be a prenuptial agreement. She probably got whatever she could out of Alonso already. Right now, she's trying to get what she can from the house while things are still up in the air. Valerie might be more of an opportunist than a murderer."

"The son seems to have a motive for wanting his father dead." Po Po's lips tightened into a thin line. "I can't believe he doesn't even have the decency to wait a few days before he goes car shopping."

"Let's not be too hasty. We don't know Gabriel, and maybe Linda is biased against him. For all we know, the two of them didn't get along. Could Linda benefit from Alonso's death?"

"I don't see how."

"She's been with the family for fifteen years. What if Alonso left her a gift in his will? That's not unusual for a loyal servant. How do we know she didn't speed things along?" Raina said.

"If she already waited fifteen years, why wouldn't she wait for a few more?"

"That's what I would like to know. Maybe we need to check that Linda didn't need a lump sum of cash."

"But if she needed money, she could have told Alonso. I'm sure he would have helped her out," Po Po said.

"Not if it's for a gambling debt or something equally nefarious."

"I can ask around," Po Po said. "What about the adopted daughter?"

"She works at one of the flooring stores. We can

stop by to see if she'll talk to us. Maybe she's in the will."

Raina glanced at the clock on the dash of her car. "I don't have time to play sleuth for the rest of the day. I have to go through the fire report and meet with contractors to get some price quotes. And I have a meeting with the insurance adjuster first thing in the morning."

"Manny is stopping by my place Friday evening. It's the only time slot he had. I need to figure out how to clog my bathroom sink. Maybe the Lovebirds can help."

Raina grinned. "You could always try clogging it with hairballs. Did you talk to your hacker about getting the phone number for Alonso's last caller?"

"She's working on it."

Raina had a feeling the phone conversation could be the key to unlocking this messy case. Why did Alonso stay in the kitchen, and who did he talk to? Was the caller the killer or a distraction that allowed the killer to strike?

RAINA WAS LOCKING up the center for the evening when her cell phone rang. She didn't recognize the number on the caller ID. "Hello? This is Raina Sun."

"This is Janice...Janice Tally. Can you come to my

unit? I need to talk to you," said the brittle voice on the phone.

"Give me five minutes. I need to check all the doors," Raina said and hung up. She locked the office door and made her way around the center, checking the doors and windows. Once she secured the facility, she trotted toward the elevator on the residential side of the building.

Raina hadn't seen Janice since the day of the fire, and until the phone call, she hadn't been concerned. However, the elderly woman on the phone sounded like she was in trouble.

In the hallway outside of Janice's unit, Raina smoothed her unruly black hair. She hoped this visit had nothing to do with her grandma. She didn't need any more trouble in the Janice and Po Po department. A stalemate would be nice. It would give Raina time and space to deal with the other important issues like Alonso's murder and the fire damage.

Raina knocked on the door, and Janice invited her inside the one-bedroom condo. The last time Raina visited Janice's home was shortly after her grandson's death a few years ago. Sometimes Raina wondered if she could have done something to save him.

The last two days hadn't been kind to the elderly woman. The wrinkles on her face were more pronounced. A roadmap of stress or grief? She leaned heavily on her walker when she led Raina toward the sofa in the living room.

There were no signs of tea or cookies on the coffee table. All the shades were down, feeding into the overall gloom and doom in the place. All right then. This was no social visit. Janice wanted to discuss something in private with Raina without interruptions.

Raina perched on the edge of the uncomfortable sofa while Janice resumed her spot on the wingback chair. "Is there something on your mind, Janice?"

Janice stared out into space for a long heartbeat. Her round glasses reflected the ceiling light and hid her eyes. Her blue-black Marge Simpson hair seemed to have lost its sheen. She cleared her throat. "They said Alonso Escalante's body was found in the kitchen fire."

Raina studied Janice with concern. The retiree balanced on a knife's edge. "Yes," she said slowly.

Janice closed her eyes and took several shuddering breaths.

Raina blinked at the reaction. Were Janice and Alonso more than friends? "Are you okay?" she asked softly.

Janice pulled an old-fashioned handkerchief out of her cardigan pocket and wiped her eyes. "I was hoping it was a mistake, and Alonso had been too busy to return my calls."

"How long had you two been together?" Raina asked. How did she miss this romantic relationship developing under her nose?

"Almost a year. We weren't hiding the relationship,

but we weren't public about it either. At our age, we didn't want people laughing at us. Alonso didn't care, but I was embarrassed."

"Why would anyone laugh at another chance for love?"

"Your grandma would."

Raina shook her head. "No, she wouldn't. She might make inappropriate comments, but she wouldn't laugh."

Janice leaned forward and gripped Raina's hands. "You have to find out who killed Alonso. I need to know who took him from me."

Raina suppressed her grimace and gently removed Janice's hand. "I'll try my best."

"You have to, or the police might arrest your grandma."

Raina's heart sank. Her grandma didn't kill Alonso, but she could have done something to get herself in trouble. "What do you mean?"

"When we were arguing in the kitchen, she turned on the stove. With the paper covering the burners, she might not have seen the red glow from the electrical ring. I'm not sure if she turned the stove off when she followed me into the game room."

Raina studied Janice's face, looking for her true intent. There was no sign of vindictiveness. Just concern for Po Po. Could there be hope for these two women after all? "Why did Po Po turn on the stove in the first place?"

"She was trying to prove how taping paper over the burners would prevent people from turning them on," Janice said.

"That doesn't make any sense."

"When has your grandma ever done anything that makes sense?"

Raina frowned, reviewing the details of the timeline for the murder in her mind. Detective Hopper had said Alonso died from a head wound, which meant there was no evidence of smoke inhalation in his lungs. Therefore, the fire had started after his death. Her grandma must have turned off the stovetop before following Janice into the game room. But Raina couldn't share this information with Janice to ease her concern.

"Did you talk to the police yet?" Raina asked.

Janice squirmed in her seat. "I'm sorry, but I told Detective Hopper what happened, and she wrote it down in her notebook."

"Good. You should always tell the truth. It will always come out in the end. There's no point in omitting details and getting yourself into trouble."

Janice sighed with relief. "You have eased my mind. I was so worried about getting your grandma into hot water."

Raina smirked. "I don't think you have to worry about that. She can make a mess of things on her own."

They burst out laughing, and the mood lightened in the room.

Janice pulled a sheet of paper from the pocket of her cardigan and held it out to Raina. "It looks like I have a motive for murdering Alonso." Her voice wobbled. "Take a look at this."

Raina took the letter and scanned the contents. Her eyes widened in shock. "He left you a hundred thousand dollars? Did you know he would leave you this much money?"

Janice shook her head. "No, I had no expectations. I got the letter this morning. I'm still in shock. What should I do? If I contact the lawyer, people will think I killed Alonso. Or I was in cahoots with your grandma."

"First, don't worry about my grandma. She's like a cat with multiple lives. Whatever trouble she's in, she can get out of it. But this bequest will make you a murder suspect. Do you want me to go with you when you talk to the lawyer?" Raina asked.

"Yes, that would be helpful. I'll give the law office a call tomorrow morning to get an appointment," Janice said.

Raina patted Janice's hand. "Leave the worrying to me. You should think about having some fun with this money after the funeral. After all, that's what Alonso would have wanted you to do."

Janice squeezed Raina's hand. "You think so?"

"Why else would he leave it to you? It's not a lot of money, so his heirs wouldn't resent you, but it's enough for you to have some fun."

"It's a lot of money to me."

"It's a rounding error when you consider the rest of Alonso's wealth. Don't feel bad about accepting it."

Raina felt a stab of guilt at the grateful look on Janice's face. She hoped the retiree would find some solace with her words. Her offer to go with Janice to the law firm wasn't entirely altruistic. Now that the lawyer had initiated the probate proceedings to settle Alonso's estate, Raina wanted to question the lawyer about the details of the will.

6

————

ARSON

Raina woke up early the next morning and got in a run before work. After she showered and changed, she power walked to the senior center, munching on a peanut butter and jelly sandwich. She had just logged into her computer when the insurance adjuster showed up.

Alex Kovac was a five-foot-nine brunette with blonde highlights. Probably in her late thirties. She had enough muscle tone to be an amateur athlete of some sort. She strode into the foyer of the senior center in no-nonsense black pumps. Her ivory button top and black trousers were respectable but forgettable. Even from a distance, Raina knew it would not be easy to win Alex over.

Raina strolled across the foyer to Alex, holding out her hand. "Alex? I'm Raina Sun."

They shook hands.

Alex's brown eyes swept through the foyer. She pulled out a cell phone and snapped photos of the smoke damage on the shared wall that connected the foyer to the kitchen. "Where is the source of the fire?"

Raina led her to the kitchen. Luckily, she had removed the chalk outline of the body yesterday. "Do you have a copy of the fire report?"

Alex nodded. "The report said the fire started from a roll of paper towels with an accelerant. Maybe a greasy pan."

"I've got the all-clear from the police," Raina said. "The crime scene tape keeps the senior citizens out of the kitchen. I've already got three quotes from contractors on my desk. I'll give them to you later."

They ducked under the crime scene tape and went into the kitchen. Alex snapped more photos with her cell phone.

"Is the facility still open?" Alex asked.

"We are only open for the hot meals program. Everything else is on hold for now," Raina said.

"How are you cooking meals without a kitchen?" Alex asked.

"I'm not. We're paying the Venus Café for the meals."

"Isn't it expensive?"

"Yes, it's more expensive than if we made the food on-site."

"Then why are you doing it? I thought the Town Council was cutting your budget."

"For some of the senior citizens, this might be their only hot meal for the day. I can't stop the program just because the kitchen isn't working."

Alex raised an eyebrow. "The extra cost has to come from somewhere."

"It's coming from our Christmas party fund for now. Once the kitchen is up and running, we will have to do fundraisers. Robbing Peter to pay Paul is not good fiscal behavior, but it's the best I can do for now to keep things 'normal' for our clients."

By this time, they were standing outside of the office. Raina strolled inside to grab the folder with the quotes from the contractors. When she stepped out, Alex was scribbling away on a notepad.

Raina handed copies of the quotes to Alex. "These are your copies. We would like to use Blue Diamond Construction because they can start on the work right away."

Alex flipped through the sheets of paper and frowned. "They are not the cheapest. We only pay for the cheapest price quote."

"The difference is two thousand dollars. The cheapest contractors have a waiting list. They will not get to us for at least three weeks, maybe longer. We need the use of our facility. Some of our clients come every day for multiple activities. The senior center is their entire social circle."

"But you do have the use of your facility. You told

me that yourself. You are using the rec room," Alex said.

"This is a temporary arrangement. We can't use the rec room for months while they repair the kitchen. The rec room hosts other community events throughout the year. It's a public facility. We only get to use it when it's not booked. And it takes a lot of effort to move the furniture around. We can't keep this up for months."

Raina didn't bother hiding the pleading in her voice. Some insurance companies were known to be difficult when it came to a claim payout, but this was ridiculous. Was Alex planning to nickel and dime their claim?

"Blue Diamond can't be that good if they can start right away. The good ones should have work lined up," Alex said primly.

Raina didn't mention that Blue Diamond Construction was owned by her brother-in-law, and he had made arrangements to put the senior center repairs ahead of his other paying jobs. Or that he might give them upgrades that were not listed in the quote.

"Our insurance policy included a daily loss of use per diem," Raina said. She pulled out a sheet of paper from her folder and handed it to Alex. "Here are my calculations for the loss of use amount through the construction period. I ran two calculations. One for the cheap contractor and the second for Blue Diamond. As you can see, you will pay us fewer days with Blue Diamond for loss of use, so this would make up for the two thousand dollars upfront."

Alex shoved the paper onto her clipboard without glancing at it. "I will have to check your policy. Why was the fire suppression system turned off at the senior center?"

"The town was repairing an emergency water main leak. All the water for this block was turned off. We only found out about the construction work that morning."

"And yet, you decided to hold a potluck on the same day when you knew the fire suppression system would be out."

Raina bristled at Alex's tone. "The potluck had been planned for weeks. I figured it wouldn't be an issue if we didn't use the kitchen. I sent out a newsletter as soon as I got the news about the emergency repair and had someone post flyers around the kitchen. Everyone was supposed to cook or warm their food at home." There was a hint of steel in Raina's voice, but she didn't bother hiding it.

"And yet someone cooked in the kitchen."

Raina clamped her mouth shut to keep from over-explaining the situation. She didn't want to tell the insurance adjuster that the fire was a cover-up for a murder. She took a deep breath, praying for patience.

"I didn't realize I needed to hire a bouncer to keep

people away from the kitchen," Raina said through gritted teeth.

Alex sighed, clearly put out. "As I said, I will have to check the policy to see what is actually covered."

"Can I let Blue Diamond start on the repairs? Will you send me a check for the entire amount, or will I be submitting receipts for reimbursement?" Raina asked, pushing for a commitment of any sort.

She couldn't wait for weeks for an answer from the insurance company. While her brother-in-law might be willing to start the repairs without a deposit, she had no money to pay him if the insurance denied the claim.

Alex gave her a false apologetic smile. "I will have to get back to you. We might not cover anything at all if this is arson."

Raina was still fuming over the meeting with the insurance adjuster when she met her grandma at the Venus Café for lunch. The green bungalow had been converted to retail space years ago and was within walking distance from the senior center.

The cafe had floor-to-ceiling murals of naked nymphs frolicking in a forest with gentlemen in Victorian suits and top hats. Long flowing hair, leaves, and berries strategically covered the lady parts.

At Raina's suggestion, the owners had converted

the restaurant to cafeteria-style dining and streamlined the menu to a choice of ten standard items and a daily special. This reduced the overhead costs and made the café profitable enough for them to close one day a week.

Using her employee discount, Raina and Po Po ordered their usual, grabbed their drinks, and secured a table before the bus person had a chance to clear it. Raina took care of the mess and dropped the dirty dishes and glasses in the tray by the kitchen door.

She scanned the dining area, looking for eavesdroppers. Everyone seemed to be focused on the conversation in front of them. Good. The fire at the senior center was starting to look complicated. She didn't want someone to overhear them and report back to Alex. She told her grandma what happened with the insurance adjuster.

"Did the insurance adjuster really say arson?" Po Po asked with incongruity.

Raina nodded. "I was expecting her to deny a line item or two, but I didn't expect she would deny the entire claim. She isn't a people's person, so no small talk. I offered her numbers and calculations, and she didn't like that either. I'm not sure how to get through to her. Does she think we would profit from the claim? It doesn't make any sense."

"Actually it does," Po Po said. "In Chinatown, sometimes a business would burn down, especially if it was no longer profitable or at the end of the lease. The owners would pocket the money and walk away from the business."

"I thought this only happened when the owners refused to give the triad protection money."

"And that too. There are many reasons for a fire that have nothing to do with accidents."

"Wait a minute. Do you think Alex is suspicious because I'm Chinese?" Raina had experienced racism a handful of times, but they were usually rare occurrences.

Po Po burst out laughing. "Rainy, I don't think your ethnic background has anything to do with this. The insurance company probably just doesn't want to pay out. What you need is leverage to get your claim processed quickly."

Raina considered her grandma's words. Leverage usually meant digging up dirt. "I guess we can do a little surveillance on Alex to see if we can find anything."

"Now we're cooking. A murder to solve and a shady inspector to put in her place." Po Po rubbed her hands together and beamed broadly. "I'm glad you didn't follow Matthew to China. Just me and you and some quality girl time."

"What quality girl time?" Brenda Sullivan asked, sliding a plate of spaghetti and meatballs in front of Po Po. She set the pastrami sandwich with a side of fries in front of Raina.

Brenda Sullivan was the co-owner of the Venus

Café. Raina had filled in at the café for Brenda while she was on maternity leave. Now that her little girl was a toddler, Raina still worked at the café one day a week to give the new mom more time with her baby.

"Rainy and I are playing Sherlock and Watson again," Po Po said, grabbing a fry off of Raina's plate.

Brenda raised an eyebrow and set down a bottle of ketchup. "The fire at the senior center?"

"What are the rumors swirling around town?" Raina asked.

"Not much. Folks are pointing fingers at either the son or the ex-wife," Brenda said.

"Valerie claims she is still married to Alonso," Raina said.

"Alonso didn't seem like the kind of man who lied about his marital status. He had bought dates here before," Brenda said.

"No, she's not. I stopped by the City Clerk's office today," Po Po said. "I found the divorce judgment."

Raina gaped at her grandma. "You did legwork?"

Po Po grabbed another fry. "I knew you were busy with paperwork and the insurance adjuster."

"Good job," Raina said to Po Po. She switched her attention to Brenda. "Did Alonso bring a special lady friend to the cafe lately?" she asked, thinking about Janice.

Brenda frowned. "Since his adopted daughter, Flora, came back to town, he had been busy spending time with her. They came for lunch once a week. They had lunch here the day Alonso died. The young woman must be terribly upset."

Raina gave her grandma a sideways glance. Flora was near the scene of the crime. Could she have hung around after lunch to sneak into the senior center later?

"So is that a yes, Raina?" Brenda asked, breaking into Raina's thoughts.

"Sorry, I was gathering wool. What did you say?" Raina asked.

"Can you babysit Gracie on Friday? Our regular babysitter got sick, and I'm working at the cafe," Brenda said. Gracie was Brenda's toddler.

"I would love to, but I have my shift at the senior center," Raina said.

"I can do it," Po Po said.

Brenda and Raina shared a look. Po Po wasn't your average grandmother. After her husband's business took off, she had hired help. It had been decades since she last gave a baby a bottle.

The cafe owner licked her lower lip. "Gracie is still in diapers. Are you okay with diapers?"

"No problem. Rainy will be downstairs at the senior center. I'll just give her a call and she can come up to my condo," Po Po said.

Raina groaned inwardly. In other words, she could expect several phone calls. She might as well do the babysitting herself.

Brenda glanced at Raina and suppressed a chuckle.

"That would be fantastic. Thank you, ladies." She left their table to return to the cash register. "Dessert is on the house."

Raina and Po Po spent the next few minutes devouring their meals. When Po Po reached for a fry again, Raina playful slapped her hand away. "Next time you should order your own fries."

"I'll give you some of my spaghetti," Po Po said.

Raina made a spot for the spaghetti on her plate and pushed it toward her grandma. Po Po scooped some spaghetti over and cleared out the fries on Raina's plate.

"Hey!" Raina said, grabbing at her plate. "Now that's playing dirty." There was a hint of laughter in her voice.

"So I'm a pig," Po Po said.

"Your indigestion will catch up with you," Raina said. She didn't care for the fries or their calories. "What were we talking about before Brenda came?"

"Digging up dirt on the insurance adjuster," Po Po said, twirling a fry in the spaghetti sauce.

"I hate the idea of twisting Alex's arm to get her to do the right thing. It's a delicate line that I'm walking," Raina said. "On one hand, there is a murder investigation. The fire probably was intentionally set to hide the body or the murder weapon. This is arson. But on the other hand, the insurance only pays for accidents."

"You're definitely in a pickle," Po Po said. "What does the fire report say?"

"Just that the fire was started by a roll of paper towels," Raina said. "He mentioned finding a body, but nothing else about the death. That would be in the coroner's report."

"And Alex wouldn't have access to an ongoing police investigation," Po Po said. "She will have to prove it's arson. It's probably a tough act, hoping you'll take whatever she offers later without argument."

Raina hoped Po Po was right. She could handle a negotiation, but if Alex had something more devious in mind, that was a whole different situation. Now how could she give herself some leverage against the insurance adjuster without going over to the dark side?

7

MAN-CHILD

After lunch, Po Po went back to her condo to put the finishing touch on Operation Clogger. Manny Díaz was coming over to fix Po Po's plumbing later in the evening.

Raina strolled home to get her car. She signed Manny Díaz's signature with a flourish on the sympathy card she had set aside for him. She studied her handiwork. Not bad. Now she had an excuse for returning to Alonso's mansion. Hopefully, she wouldn't run into Valerie again.

The drive was uneventful. Raina spent the time reviewing what she knew of the murder investigation. She hadn't told her grandma about Janice Tally's inheritance and relationship with Alonso during lunch. Keeping the secret weighed heavily on Raina's mind. If Po Po knew about this, would she give Janice a fair shake? Or would she automatically assume her arch nemesis was guilty of murder?

When Raina knocked at the front door of the mansion, Linda opened it with a wide smile. Her blonde curls still hung loose and framed her face like a lion's mane, but the sparkle in her eyes was anything but predatory. They were filled with hope and joy.

Raina cocked her head and studied the housekeeper. "Did Alonso leave you money?"

Linda's smile grew even wider. "How do you know?"

"A friend of mine also found out he left her money. I'm assuming his lawyer has been contacting his heirs in the last day or two."

"I have enough to get a small condo for myself."

Raina blinked. A small condo in California was several hundred thousand dollars. Did Linda know Alonso would leave her money? Probably not. When they had spoken after Alonso's death, Linda had been stressed about her job and living situation. "Congratulations. This is good news. When are you leaving?"

"Not until I am told to pack my bags. Mr. Gabriel rarely comes to the kitchen. I just have to stock the refrigerator with microwavable food. He's even easier to care for than Mr. Alonso."

"Is Gabriel here?," Raina asked. "I would like to talk to him." She held out the sympathy card. "I have another one for him."

"He's in the garage washing his new sports car. I'll show you where it is," Linda said.

As they strolled past the living room, Raina paused at the entryway. "What happened to the TV?"

Linda shrugged. "Things are disappearing from the house. Maybe Mr. Gabriel needs money. I don't know if he is still getting his allowance. And it might take some time to get his inheritance."

"Are you sure this isn't the work of Valerie?" Raina asked.

Linda shrugged again. "I don't know, and I don't care. If Mr. Gabriel isn't worried about it, then I'm not losing sleep over it. I forgot to tell you about the smoked brisket last time."

"The one that Alonso was supposed to bring to the potluck? What about it?" Raina asked.

"It disappeared. I can't find it anywhere," Linda said.

"What do you mean, disappeared?"

"I put the brisket in a Pyrex container and covered it with foil. I put the whole thing in the oven to keep it warm for Mr. Alonso. I left the lid on the counter with a note about the brisket in the oven and went to my room to shower."

"Was this before or after you called Alonso about the brisket?"

"Before I called. In the note, I asked Mr. Alonso to turn off the oven when he took the container out."

"And when did the brisket disappear?"

Linda shrugged. "I don't know. The oven was still on when I came back to the kitchen. I turned it off, but I didn't open the oven. I wanted to keep the heat inside. I called Mr. Alonso but got his voicemail. I had my dinner while watching a TV show, and then the police showed up."

"When did you remember to check the oven?"

"After the police left. I opened the oven, and there was nothing inside."

"Did Gabriel eat it?" Raina asked.

"I don't think so. If he did, where is the container? It's not in his room."

"The house is pretty big. Maybe it's in one of the other rooms."

"The maid service hasn't found it yet. I don't think it's in the house."

Next to the kitchen, they stepped through a doorway and out to the garage.

Raina's jaw dropped. The finished garage was a six-car tandem monstrosity that could double as a banquet hall. The floor had an epoxy coating that gave it a light tan color. Wood paneling lined the walls along with shelves, hooks, and other doohickeys that would have made her husband salivate on sight. The garage doors were rolled up, letting in sunlight and the sound of bubbling water from the fountain in the courtyard next to the kitchen.

In one corner was Alonso's old white Toyota Camry. And smack in the middle was a shiny red two-seater with tan leather seats—a Lexus to go by the logo on the car. Raina was surprised a car dealer sold the vehicle to Gabriel based on a potential inheritance. He was polishing the headlight with a soft white cloth.

"Mr. Gabriel, someone is here to see you. A friend of your father," Linda called out from the doorway. She gestured for Raina to go in and left.

"I'm busy. Tell the person to come back later," Gabriel said without glancing up.

Raina stepped into the garage. "Hi, I'm Raina Sun. Sorry to bother you, but I want to give my condolences. Alonso was a well-respected member of our community." She held out the sympathy card.

Gabriel's head jerked up at the sound of Raina's voice. He was a younger version of Alonso—olive skin, jet-black hair, and deep brown eyes. He also carried an extra thirty pounds, and the curve on his spine indicated he spent a lot of time sitting in front of the computer or TV. Since Raina knew he didn't work, she assumed the hunch came from playing video games.

He took the card and looked at the signature. "Who is this guy?"

"Your dad's former business partner."

Gabriel folded the card in half and tucked it into the back pocket of his shorts. "Message received. You can go now." He returned to polishing his headlight.

Raina bristled at his dismissive tone. What did Alonso do to deserve such a son? "I also came by to warn you."

"I don't even know you." His tone implied that she was exaggerating.

"I came as a favor for Alonso. The police are looking into Alonso's death."

Gabriel straightened. Something finally got his attention. "Why would they do that? My old man died from a fire. Accidents happen all the time."

"Not in this case. They didn't find any signs of smoke inhalation in Alonso's lungs."

"Oookay," Gabriel said.

"He died before the fire started."

His brow furled. "I still don't get it."

"This means somebody killed your dad and started a fire to hide it." Raina studied his face, looking for a reaction.

He blinked in confusion. "That makes no sense. The old man had no enemies. And he spent most of his time at the senior center. What kind of trouble could happen there with a bunch of old people?"

Raina suppressed the urge to lecture him on respecting the elderly. Good thing her grandma wasn't with her, or she might smack him. "What about you? Did you want Alonso dead?"

Gabriel gaped at her. "That's crazy talk. He was my dad. Why would I want him dead?"

Raina waved a hand in the air. "So you can inherit all this."

"And deal with it all? No thanks. I had a good thing going until the old man died on me. Now I got a lawyer calling about paperwork. And other people calling about the business. They must think I have nothing to do all day. And my old stepmom calling about the furniture. What do I care? It's old stuff."

Raina studied Gabriel. He was in his early thirties, which meant Alonso had his son later in life and probably spoiled him terribly. The man seemed unprepared for the real world. Or maybe he was a talented actor.

"Will you fire Linda? She thinks you'll get rid of her when you sell the house," Raina said.

"No! She's been part of the family since forever. I can't get rid of her. Who will do my laundry and cook my food? She's the only mother I ever had."

"Maybe you should tell her that. She thought she would need to find another place to live. And Valerie has been bossing Linda around."

Gabriel paused for a long moment as if absorbing Raina's words. He nodded to himself, and Raina hoped he took her words to heart. He was like a child in a man's body. Or maybe he was a self-centered brat.

"How is my old stepmom getting into the house?" he finally asked.

Raina shrugged. "Could Flora have given Valerie a key?"

Gabriel thought about Raina's words for a moment. "Linda needs to get someone to change the locks."

"How do you feel about Flora?"

"What do you mean? My old man adopted her, but

she's not my sister. She showed up a few months ago and started spending time with him."

"Were you jealous of the relationship?"

"Nah. I'm his only son. The old man was big on machismo because he grew up in the old country. With Flora around, he was too distracted to get on my case about working at the family business."

"Why aren't you interested in following in your father's footsteps?"

"I tried it for two summers, and it gave me anxiety. I was on medication. I don't like dealing with people. I can't read their emotions. People don't say what they want. They expect me to be a mind reader. I can't deal with that."

Raina studied Gabriel for a long moment, wondering if he might have Asperger syndrome. It would explain his awkward reaction to his father's death and his inability to handle adulting. "You're probably the prime suspect. If you haven't already, call the lawyer back and ask for a referral to a lawyer that can help you. The police will want to question you."

"They already did. And I don't think they will come back." Gabriel swallowed, his Adam's apple bobbing up and down. "I would give anything to have the old man back. He was supposed to show me the ropes someday. Now I have no one." His voice cracked, and he shifted his gaze as if embarrassed by the emotion.

When Raina left the Escalante mansion, she was more confused than ever. With both Gabriel and Linda crossed off the suspect list, that left only the ex-wife, the adopted daughter, and the former business partner. However, all three suspects probably weren't on the inheritance list.

Maybe money wasn't the motive for the murder. What could these three suspects gain from murdering Alonso? Revenge? Her head throbbed. Hopefully, she would get some answers from Manny Díaz when he came over to fix her grandma's plumbing later in the evening.

8

———

SWEET AMBUSH

aina returned to the senior center to find it in shambles. Before the college students had finished removing the furniture for the hot meal program, the Design Guild had arrived to set up the recreation room for their show over the weekend. The Guild's coordinator was screaming at the poor students. Raina mentally rolled up her sleeves and dove into the maelstrom.

An hour later, she sent the students home and made a mental note to bake some goodies for them. The double doors that connected the rec room to the senior center were firmly locked for the next few days. They would have to hand out bag lunches in the foyer until they could use the rec room again.

At her desk, Raina rubbed her temples. *The insurance money better come through soon,* she thought. She took a Tylenol and pulled out the fancy box of chocolate truffles from the filing cabinet. It was too early for wine, but there were other ways to self-medicate. She opened the budget spreadsheet and settled in for the rest of her shift.

Knock! Knock!

Raina glanced up from the spreadsheet on the computer to the doorway of her tiny office.

A redhead a few years younger than Raina was standing at her door. She was about five foot four in her espadrille wedges. Her T-shirt and shorts matched Raina's in the clean but wrinkled category. Maybe they were both bosom buddies in a different lifetime.

Raina glanced at the clock display on the corner of her computer. One hour before Operation Clogger. Hopefully, this would take less than thirty minutes. She didn't want her grandma alone with Manny Díaz in her condo without backup. The Lovebirds had to leave town, but they would watch the show through a mobile app. Po Po had scattered several wireless cameras throughout her condo. If things went sideways, the Lovebirds would call the police.

She hit the save button and closed the spreadsheet on her computer. She waved the redhead in, hoping she wasn't from the Design Guild. "How can I help you?"

The woman stepped inside, holding out her hand. "Hi, are you Raina Sun? My name is Flora, Alonso Escalante's daughter." On closer inspection, Raina saw that her face and body were mostly covered by freck-les, the bane of most redheads.

Raina shook Flora's hand and gestured for her to take the folding metal seat in front of the desk. This must be her lucky day. She had planned to track down the elusive adopted daughter tomorrow afternoon.

Flora sat down and twisted the hem of her T-shirt. "I want to thank you for dropping off the sympathy cards. It's good to know that Dad had friends who care about his passing, especially since our family...is less vocal about our grief."

Raina wasn't sure how to respond. From what the housekeeper had told her, the Escalante family—except for Flora—were already spending Alonso's money. But greedy relatives weren't the same thing as a murderer. "We will miss Alonso around here."

Flora fidgeted with her T-shirt again. "This will sound weird, but can you show me around? Dad spent so many happy hours here that I want to feel his presence."

Raina got up from her desk. "Let's go. I need to stretch my legs. I've been doing paperwork for the last hour."

They strode out of Raina's office and back into the foyer.

Raina led them into the game room. The smoky smell from the fire was mostly gone. "Here's where the old coots hang out most of the day. One or two of them have a police scanner, so sometimes it is on in the background like a radio."

Flora glanced around the room with wide eyes. "Is that what Dad did here? Listen to the police scanner?"

"That's actually my grandma and her friends. Alonso usually hung out with Janice and her friends. They play bridge or board games." Raina gave Flora a wry smile. "It's like high school here. Everyone has their clique."

Flora gaped at Raina. "Seriously? I thought older people were more...dignified."

Raina rolled her eyes. "That's what they want us to believe. Sometimes this job is like herding toddlers, and other times it's like counseling hormonal high school students. And every one of them has decades on me."

They burst out laughing. Raina felt the tension of the afternoon drain away. Sometimes she forgot how good it felt to be around someone her age.

Flora wiped a tear from her blue eyes. "Sounds like a riot. Though I wouldn't have the patience to handle it."

Raina gave Flora a sideways glance. "How do you like working in the family business? I'm surprised Gabriel isn't upset with your sudden return to town."

"At first, everyone tiptoed around me because I was the boss's daughter. Then after a while, they got used to it, especially since dad didn't show me any favors at work. As for Gabriel"—Flora shrugged—"he's just waiting for his big payday. As long as I don't get in the way of that, he doesn't care."

"What happens to the business now?" Raina asked.

"Since Dad's retirement, there is an operation manager that oversees the entire business. And each store has a store manager. The business can pretty much run itself with a little oversight from Gabriel."

"It doesn't sound like he's interested in the business at all. Said it gave him anxiety." Raina studied Flora. For a moment, she'd forgotten that she was in the presence of a murder suspect. "Will you provide the oversight on the business?"

Flora's smile wobbled. "I doubt it. I'm not in the will. I'm not even his biological daughter." She blushed as if she were embarrassed to reveal the truth.

Raina frowned. "Why aren't you in the will? It shouldn't matter whether you're his biological daughter or not. He had adopted you, so you're family." And it didn't make any sense that Alonso left money to his housekeeper but nothing for the daughter of his heart.

Flora blinked rapidly. Tears pooled at the corner of her eyes. When she could finally speak, it was thick with emotion. "Thank you. You have no idea how much your words mean to me."

Raina patted Flora's shoulder. "Family comes in many different forms, and sometimes in an unexpected way."

Flora nodded. "Alonso was the only father figure in

my life. He was my mother's second husband. None of the others ever stuck around."

Raina felt a twinge of guilt for her nosy questions, but the money was her only lead in the murder investigation. "It's so strange. He adopted you and welcomed you with open arms. And yet, he left you nothing."

"I told Dad not to. He wanted to change his will when I first came back to town, but I didn't think it would sit well with Gabriel. And honestly, that's not what I wanted. I just got out of a bad marriage, and I wanted to be around my own people."

"And now, it's too late for changes," Raina said. "I'm sorry." Her words sounded inadequate even to her own ears. Without a stake in the inheritance, Flora had no motive for killing Alonso.

Flora gave Raina a shaky smile. "Don't worry about me. I will be okay, but my mom..." She shook her head. "She never wanted a divorce, but she was forced into it."

"What happened? I heard she had an affair with Manny."

"It wasn't an affair. More like an ambush. Manny got Mom drunk one night, and he arranged for Dad to find them the next morning."

"Then what happened?"

"They got divorced."

"But I thought you said Valerie was forced into it? How can you force someone to sign divorce papers?"

"It was the prenuptial agreement. Mom got to keep

the settlement. If she had fought the divorce proceed-ings, Dad had threatened to withhold the money. And with a young child…" Flora shrugged. "Mom didn't have much of a choice. And he'd paid child support for me all these years, which was why Mom thought she still had a chance with him."

"But Valerie remarried…more than once."

"She was trying to make him jealous. It never worked."

Flora was a child when Alonso and Valerie divorced. Her mom must have told Flora this story later when she became a teen or adult. And it laid the blame entirely on Manny. Raina was surprised there were no hard feelings against the former business partner.

9

OPERATION CLOGGER

Raina locked the office and checked the locks for the senior center. She ran upstairs for Operation Clogger. With twenty minutes until showtime, she was cutting it close. As Raina hurried to her grandma's condo unit, she squinted at the open door at the end of the hallway. Was that Manny Díaz's door? Raina glanced at the number on her right and counted the doors to the open door. Yikes! It was Manny's door. And he was coming out.

There was no place to hide in the corridor. Raina spun on her heel and ran, hoping to hide in the stairwell next to the elevator. Manny didn't seem like the type to take the stairs just for the exercise.

Raina's heart raced, and her breaths came out in jagged puffs that echoed in the metal and concrete space. A few minutes later, her cell phone dinged with an incoming message. It was from her grandma.

MANNY IS HERE. WHERE ARE YOU?

Raina cursed. Manny had to be one of those people who got to places super early. Her hands flew across the screen.

SAW MANNY COMING OUT OF HIS CONDO. I RAN THE OPPOSITE WAY, SO NOW I'M HIDING IN THE STAIRS.

Raina pushed open the metal door and jogged to her grandma's condo. Her leg muscles ached. At this rate, she would be useless by the time she got inside the condo. Forget about fending off an attack. She would be lucky to catch her breath.

She whipped out her cell phone and texted her grandma.

I'M OUTSIDE YOUR DOOR.

Po Po's front door opened silently. She gestured for Raina to come inside.

Raina tiptoed into the living room. On her left were the two bedrooms with a bathroom between them. Through the doorway of the bathroom, Raina saw a pair of hairy white legs. Manny was under the sink.

Po Po strolled across the living room and stood in front of the bathroom entryway, providing what cover she could with her petite frame.

As Raina crab-walked along the wall to the spare bedroom, sweat ran down her face and back. Her heart hadn't gotten a chance to slow down from her mad dash from the stairwell. She slipped inside the room and exhaled in relief. She closed the door but left a two-inch gap for eavesdropping.

Raina was in place to provide backup. The rest was her grandma's show. She crossed her fingers, hoping the questioning would run smoothly. When it came to her grandma, sometimes things could go off on a tangent or explode in her face.

Po Po cleared her throat and asked in an overly loud voice, "How did you and Alonso get over your disagreement? Did he leave you money in his will?"

Manny grunted. There was the sound of banging like he was hitting the pipe. "Why would he leave me money?"

"Alonso couldn't take the money with him. I'm assuming he left it to the people who needed money. And you were his best friend. It would make sense for him to help you out. It's not like you are rolling in the dough..."

Raina slapped her forehead. Leave it to her grandma to mention the humiliating fact that Manny didn't save enough money for his retirement.

"Geez, thanks for pointing that out," Manny said. "Nothing like getting kicked when I'm down."

"Sorry," Po Po mumbled. "Alonso had so much money, and you... What happened? Why did you sell your half of the business to Alonso?"

Manny sighed audibly. There was a shuffling noise, and a metal tool hitting another metal tool. "My wife got sick. We had health insurance, but it was a crappy plan with high deductibles and copays. At the time, the business wasn't worth much—just one store. We were barely getting enough business to cover our overhead. Alonso was willing to buy me out and let me stay as an employee." His voice seemed to come from above Raina, which meant he was standing.

Raina tensed. With Manny in an upright position, he could quickly whack her grandma in the head with a wrench.

"Sounds like a good deal. Without the stress of being a business owner and instant cash to pay the bills," Po Po said.

"I thought so too, until Alonso filed a patent for the glue that I invented for the wood flooring," Manny said. "And because I was now an employee, whatever I did during work time belonged to the company. Alonso didn't even offer me a small share for the glue. I understood the terms of my employment, but come on, he was supposed to be my best friend. Couldn't he have given me a small token for the glue? I would have been happy with ten percent."

"If he had offered you a share of the glue, it would have set a precedent with the other employees," Po Po said. As the wife of a business owner, her grandma understood the risks involved. "Did he give you a big bonus for it?"

There was a long pause.

Sweat continued to bead down Raina's back. The muscles on her legs were tight from the fight or flight tension coursing through her body. If Po Po didn't get on with the questions, Raina might have to sit down. The lush carpet looked just as appealing as the full-size bed a few feet away. If Manny continued to be this talkative, then her grandma didn't need a bodyguard.

Raina's ears perked at the sounds of splashing and squishing. Was Manny plunging the toilet?

"Yeah, he gave me a nice bonus, but the glue went on to make Alonso millions when he sold it to Ape Glue. Then he used the money to expand the business into a chain. I taught him everything he knew about the flooring business," Manny said.

"You were definitely hosed," Po Po said, once again pointing out Manny's misfortune. "How did you end up in prison?"

"I stole money from the company."

Po Po gasped. There was a Chinese proverb that literally translated to eating someone's rice and flipping the bowl over afterward. This proverb was the equivalent to biting the hand that feeds you. Her grandma was big on loyalty.

"Hey, he wouldn't share. It wasn't my fault." There was a hint of defensiveness in Manny's voice.

Raina stepped out of the spare room and stood next to her grandma. If her grandma continued to agitate Manny, he might clam up.

"Hi, Manny. I didn't even know you were here." Raina turned to address Po Po. "What's for dinner?" The question was an excuse to get rid of her grandma. Po Po burnt her last dish decades ago when her husband's shipping business took off, and she hired a cook.

Po Po gave Raina a deadpan stare, knowing full well what Raina was up to. "Let me consult my take-out menus." She turned in a huff and flounced into the kitchen like a teenager.

Manny watched her grandma with a bemused expression on his face. "She can wear a man down and eat him up for dinner." There was no malice in his voice. "She's too hot to handle."

Raina chuckled. "If you want to take her off my hands, you are welcome to try." She threw in the last comment to keep the mood light. There was no way she would welcome a potential murderer in her grandma's life until he got the all-clear.

Manny rubbed his long fingers on his chin, considering Raina's words. He shook his head. "No, she would be the death of me."

They both burst out laughing. Po Po banged something in the kitchen to let them know she heard their comments, which set off another round of laughter.

Raina glanced at the toilet. It was brown and clogged with toilet paper and strips of newspaper. Her grandma must have used up the entire bottle of chocolate sauce.

Manny followed Raina's gaze. He lowered his voice. "I know this is a setup."

Raina's eyes widened. They were so busted. Did he throw in lies to confuse them? She licked her lower lip. "A setup for what?"

"Bonnie wants to spend time with me. I know she's got the hots for me. I can feel her eyes following my every move in the game room."

Raina stared at Manny's face. Was he for real? There was no mistaking the hint of self-satisfaction in his voice or the tilt of his head like a puffed-up rooster. She bit the inside of her cheek and shifted her gaze back to the toilet. When she finally suppressed the urge to laugh, she said, "I thought you were already involved with someone. You were seen with Valerie Escalante."

Manny rested his elbow on top of the plunger and hooked the thumb of the other hand in his belt loop. "I had an affair with Valerie years ago to get back at Alonso. She called after Alonso's death because she wanted my opinion on the value of a few pieces at the mansion. Before settling into plumbing, I worked on estate sales for a while."

Raina narrowed her eyes in mock suspicion. "This thing between you and Valerie—is it over? I don't want my grandma to get hurt."

"Over and done. We are friends now."

Raina studied Manny. Maybe he was oblivious to his precarious situation. "But you broke up her marriage. Are you sure she has forgiven you? She might still be holding a grudge."

Manny waved aside Raina's concern. "Not much she can do about it now. Alonso is dead." There was no glee or malice in his tone. Maybe he had forgiven Alonso before the fire incident.

"Valerie claims she is still married to Alonso, but there is a divorce decree. How is she entitled to the things in the house?"

Manny shrugged. "She bought most of the items during their marriage. Maybe she felt like they belong to her. And Gabriel doesn't seem to be attached to the things in the house."

Raina wasn't so sure about that. Though Gabriel might think the house was too big, the process of actually selling the place and moving would be too stressful for him. Maybe Linda could manage the house sale.

"How did you resolve your animosity toward Alonso?" Raina asked.

The back of Manny's eyes shifted like someone closed the curtains. "You're asking a lot of questions about Alonso. This has nothing to do with your grandma's interest in me, does it?"

"Oh, she's interested," Raina lied with a straight face. She kicked the twinge of guilt aside. "But I want to make sure she wouldn't have to visit you in a prison cell."

"I already told you, I didn't kill him." Manny's words were heartfelt. "What do I need to do to convince you of this?"

"Manny, I am only trying to help. The police suspect it's an insider job—someone from the senior center. You're one of us. You're part of the family. I don't want anything to happen to you."

As the words left Raina's mouth, she realized it was true. These retirees were her responsibility. It wasn't part of her job description, but they were like an extension of her family.

Manny's face flushed. He appeared to be moved by Raina's words. He averted his face and began plunging the toilet again.

Raina's thoughts drifted back to her conversations with the suspects. They all claimed to have no motive for murdering Alonso, but no one had an alibi. What was she missing?

"I broke up Alonso's marriage with Valerie," Manny said. "And later, he paid for my son's college and medical school under the guise of scholarships. When I found out about the fake scholarships, I figured we were squared. That probably would have been my share from the glue patent. Unlike Alonso, I would have taken the money and run instead of risking it on new stores. I have forgiven him."

Raina believed him. Even though Manny didn't have millions like Alonso did, Manny still ended up okay. His son was a doctor, and he had a second home in Mexico next to his sister's house. He didn't seem like someone who wanted revenge for an old grudge. "How did you find out about the fake scholarship?"

"When my son told me that he got the free ride for medical school. It was maybe a couple years ago. I confronted Alonso about it. My son is good, but he's not *that* good. A father knows these things."

"What were you doing before the fire?"

"I was outside in the garden, talking to Valerie," Manny said. "Then I went back to my unit. I passed Toshi Manohar in the hallway outside my door. We spoke for a while about the upcoming golfing tournament, and then the fire alarms went off."

Raina's jaw dropped. "You had an alibi all along? Why didn't you say so?" And Valerie was near the scene of the crime? Could she have come into the kitchen through the side exit, seen Alonso, and started an argument that led to his death?

Manny flushed the toilet and turned to face Raina. "I said I had nothing to do with—"

The toilet exploded. Raw sewage leaped up into the air. Clumps of toilet paper and other unmentionables splattered Raina's face and body. She gagged and staggered into the living room. Liquid overflowed onto the carpet.

Po Po ran over. "What's happening?"

"I think you clogged the branch line," Manny said. He was down on all fours, turning off the valves behind the toilet. "I need the keys to check on the branch line in the basement of the building. I hope this didn't back up to the other units."

Raina pulled out the key and handed it to Manny. The basement was nothing more than a giant concrete box under the condo complex that housed all the mechanical, electrical, and plumbing that made the building habitable. It was off-limits to the residents.

Manny took off, his long thin legs working at top speed. The front door slammed closed in his wake.

Po Po turned pale like someone hit her on the stomach. "Oh, sh—"

"Grab some old towels or sheets. You don't want this all over the living room," Raina said. "And get me a pair of shoes or sandals and a change of clothes. If you have wipes, please get them. I don't want to traipse all over the condo with this stuff on me."

Po Po turned and flew into the spare bedroom.

Raina wiped at the liquid dripping down the tip of her nose and smeared it on her even filthier T-shirt. She swallowed the bile rising from the back of her throat and breathed through her mouth. Her nose couldn't take the smell anymore.

Why in the world did she let her grandma plan this

operation? While she had gotten the information she needed from Manny, she also had another crisis on her hands if the sewage backed up to the other units. And how could she explain this to the HOA? She was an idiot for taking this job.

10

BROKEN TREE

After Manny worked his magic in the basement, they found three additional condo units with exploding toilets. Po Po apologized profusely and got the neighbors' information for her homeowner's insurance. Raina and Po Po opened the windows in the condo and left for Raina's house. Her grandma would call a cleaning service in the morning.

After Raina showered and got into her comfy pajamas, she felt human again. She went downstairs to find her grandma still on the phone with Uncle Anthony, explaining the exploding toilet incident. Even from a distance, she could hear her eldest uncle screaming on the phone line and threatening to throw her grandma into the loony bin.

Raina pulled out the ingredients to make toffee and chocolate chip cookies. She could understand her uncle's anger. Every time her grandma got into trouble, she called her eldest son, expecting him to take care of it—from doing paperwork to writing a check. Maybe this was why Uncle Anthony was going bald.

She pulled the first batch of cookies out from the oven and left them on the countertop to cool. The second batch was for the college students. When the oven timer went off for the second time, she had a fresh pot of rooibos tea and a plate of cookies at the kitchen table.

Po Po finished her conversation and leaned back onto her chair like she just finished running a marathon.

Raina poured her grandma tea. Po Po tapped on the table three times with her index and middle fingers.

Tap. Tap. Tap.

The ancient custom of saying thank you without words in a tea ceremony.

"Don't forget to call Brenda. She will have to drop Gracie off here in the morning," Raina said.

Po Po straightened. "What?"

"You promised to babysit Brenda's toddler when we were at the Venus Café."

Po Po's eyes widened. "But...I have so much to do tomorrow, and you will be at work."

"And Brenda has to be at the café. You'll be fine. After all, you raised six kids." Raina didn't bother hiding her amusement. At least she wouldn't have to run up and down the senior complex tomorrow. It was the only positive thing that came from tonight's mishap.

The next morning, Raina crept out her front door, bypassing the kitchen. Po Po was already awake, enjoying her usual breakfast of tea and toast. Raina didn't want to be around when Brenda dropped off Gracie. As much as Raina would love to see the toddler, she didn't want to be late for work.

The first hour at the senior center flew by. Luckily, the sewer backup was Po Po's problem, so Raina didn't have to deal with it. She left the plate of cookies for the students on the table in the foyer. The students had already gotten the instructions to hand out the bag lunches for the hot meal program.

Raina left a message for Alex Kovac to call her back about the insurance claim. She was responding to the Town Council about the status of the fire repairs when Janice knocked on her door.

"I have an appointment with Ms. Goldberg at eleven. Are you still taking me there?" Janice said from the doorway.

Raina glanced at the clock display on the corner of the computer. "Yes, but I better grab a snack before-hand. It will be a late lunch at this rate." She could always return to the paperwork later. She stood up and grabbed her purse from the drawer on her desk. "Have you eaten anything yet? I don't want you to faint from hunger."

Janice shook her head. "I'm too nervous to eat. I kept pinching myself all morning. This doesn't feel real."

"Come on. Let's grab a pastry from the Venus Café. I could do with an iced coffee. My grandma is babysitting Gracie Sullivan right now," Raina said, locking her office door.

"You're kidding me. When is the last time Bonnie changed a diaper?" Janice asked, amused.

"Longer than I have been alive," Raina said with a cheeky grin.

Raina tucked Janice into the passenger seat of her old Honda Accord and put the walker into the trunk. Outside the Venus Café, Janice opted to wait in the car. Raina ran in and got blueberry muffins, an iced tea, and an iced coffee. They dug into their goodies during the short drive.

Goldberg and Associates was four blocks from the Venus Café. It was a walkable distance, but Raina wasn't sure Janice could make it with her little walker. And with Raina's luck, her hair would spaz out in the heat, and she would arrive looking like a walking dandelion. She parked at the curb in front of the two-story building.

The law firm had converted the colonial house into office space a few years ago. As Janice shuffled up the pathway to the front door, Raina fell half a step behind the retiree to give her more room to maneuver the walker.

The red front door opened, and Gabriel Escalante stepped out with a scowl on his face. He recognized Raina and lifted his hand as if to wave but froze when he saw Janice. His expression darkened even more.

Gabriel stalked over and stood directly in front of Janice, blocking her path. "Did you tell my father to lock up the money in a trust?"

"What are you talking about, Gabriel?" The hint of exasperation in Janice's voice was perfect—like she was talking to a naughty little boy.

Raina flanked Janice on the right and placed a hand on Janice's elbow. The old bird was trembling. "Take a deep breath, Gabriel. We just got here. What's going on?"

Gabriel gestured at the colonial building behind him. "Ms. Goldberg told me the money is locked up. I'm getting a bigger allowance, but it's not enough." He raked a hand through his hair. "How am I supposed to pay Linda to take care of me?"

"Maybe the maintenance on the house is paid out separately," Raina said, hoping she sounded reasonable. "Why would Janice have anything to do with your dad's will?"

Gabriel continued to scowl at Janice. "He talked about his new girlfriend all the time, and how she gave such wonderful advice. She has something to do with this."

"Could it be Flora's influence?" Raina said,

throwing out the comment to see how Gabriel would react.

"Who am I influencing?" said a familiar voice from behind Raina.

Gabriel's gaze shifted to a spot above Raina's shoulder. "What are you doing here?"

Raina turned to see a redhead in a pale blue sundress walking up the path toward them. With the sun glinting off her sunglasses, Flora was a vision of health and youth. Raina smoothed her hands over her T-shirt and skort, feeling underdressed.

"I have no idea. I got a call from Ms. Goldberg," Flora said, giving her adopted brother a sweet smile. "Maybe Daddy left me something too."

Raina gave Flora a sideways glance. Why was she baiting him? Was this normal sibling rivalry or something else?

"He was not your father," Gabriel said. There was a hint of anger in his voice. "Your mother married two other men after my dad. Do you call them daddy too, you little gold digger?"

Flora's hands curled into fists. "Alonso is my father. He adopted me when I was a child."

"If you meant anything to my father, why did he ignore you all these years?" Gabriel asked.

Flora shook with suppressed anger. She shoved past Gabriel and ran off, disappearing around the building.

Gabriel's jaw tightened. "I probably shouldn't have said that. I hate it when she calls him daddy."

Raina raised an eyebrow. "I thought you didn't mind that she was spending time with Alonso."

"I don't. It's the fake sweet stuff that makes me gag," Gabriel said with a grimace. "She hasn't seen my old man for more than a decade, and after a few months, she acts like she grew up with me."

"Maybe she has daddy issues," Janice chimed in for the first time.

Gabriel's gaze flickered to the retiree. "She has issues, all right, and I want nothing to do with it. She doesn't act this way with her other stepfathers. Maybe she is setting things up to challenge the will."

"Flora said your father offered to change the will to include her. She told him not to because she didn't want to upset you," Raina said.

"She came back to town, divorced and broke. The first thing she did was look my father up," Gabriel said. "Even if she didn't directly ask my old man for money, she must have known he was generous. After all, her mother is always hanging around, looking for a handout. And they have been divorced for half my life."

Raina considered his words. They made sense. Death had a way of making relatives come out of the woodwork, especially with Alonso's large estate.

"Have you made funeral arrangements?" Janice asked Gabriel. "I would like to attend."

Gabriel stared at the wrinkled face for a long

moment. His expression softened, and the scowl disappeared. "Linda is taking care of it. I'll have her call you with the information."

"Your father was a good man. I miss him," Janice said with a catch in her voice.

Gabriel patted her shoulder awkwardly. His face was pink with embarrassment. "I'm sorry about what I said. I was upset. I need to talk to Linda. She will help me figure this mess out." He turned and disappeared to the parking lot behind the building.

Once Gabriel was out of earshot, Raina whispered, "Are you okay?"

Janice nodded. "Come on. Ms. Goldberg is waiting for us."

The receptionist showed Raina into a conference room. It was once the parlor and dining room for the colonial house. The law firm had knocked down the connecting wall but kept the original wallpaper. The parlor had rich cream walls to catch the morning sun, and the dining room had robin blue walls to soothe the appetite. In the middle of the room was a large mahogany table with plush leather chairs. Oddly enough, the conference room suited the law firm.

Ms. Goldberg was in her late fifties with salt and pepper in her cornrows. She wore a cream tailored suit, a crisp red shirt, and cream ballet slippers. Her dark brown skin was unlined, except for the crow's feet at the corner of her warm brown eyes. She glanced up from the leather portfolio in front of her when Raina and Janice walked in.

They shook hands, and Janice explained Raina's presence.

Ms. Goldberg frowned, flipped through several pages on her portfolio. "Mrs. Raina Sun Louie. Here you are." She tapped on the sheet of paper. "I'm glad you came by. I needed to talk to you as well."

Raina and Janice shared a confused look.

Ms. Goldberg continued, "Alonso left a bequest for the senior center. A scholarship fund for the low-income retirees who couldn't pay for their activity fees."

Raina smiled for the first time all morning. "Alonso mentioned setting up a scholarship fund, but I didn't think he would have time to do it before...his untimely death."

Tires squealed outside the bay window. A honk. *Bang!*

Raina leaped up from her chair and hurried to the window. Across the street, wrapped around a tree trunk was a shiny red car. She staggered back from the window and fell back into the leather chair. Her breaths came out in ragged puffs. It couldn't have been Gabriel's car.

Janice reached over and touched Raina's clammy hand. "What is it, my dear? What's going on outside?"

Raina blinked at the lawyer. "What happens if Gabriel Escalante dies before he inherits the money?"

Ms. Goldberg's gaze shifted to the bay window. The wail of approaching emergency vehicles could be heard through the dual pane windows. "Then all the money goes into a trust for the senior center. And you, Raina, are one of the trustees."

Raina buried her head into her hands. Great. Another headache in the making.

Janice swiveled in her chair and peered out of the bay window. A fire truck had pulled up, blocking the scene. "What's going on out there? Is it a car accident?"

"It's Gabriel's car," Raina said through numb lips. "And I don't think he'll walk away from it."

11

SABATOGE

After settling Janice in her home, Raina strolled across the lobby of the condo complex, hoping to return to the paperwork for the fire damage. Anything to forget the disturbing image of the red car wrapped around the tree trunk. She didn't want to think about the implications of the car crash until she could do it privately.

A tall brunette ducked under the crime scene tape and slipped into the kitchen of the senior center. Was that Alex Kovac?

Raina hurried across the foyer and peered into the kitchen. The insurance adjuster wore a blue silk top and black trousers. Her hair was pulled back into a chignon. It wasn't an outfit made for sneaking around.

Alex opened and closed one cabinet after another. What was she searching for? And should Raina announce her presence?

Raina pulled out her cell phone from her purse and turned on the video recording app. Through the tiny screen, she saw Alex reached into a shelf. It was now or never.

With the cell phone held casually in her hand but pointed at Alex, Raina stepped into the kitchen. "Can I help you with something?"

Alex jerked her hand back from the cabinet. "No, I'm fine. I'm here to take more pictures. You didn't mention the contents inside your cupboards in the spreadsheets you gave me. The insurance company should give you money to replace them." Her tone was taut like she was nervous.

Liar, liar, Raina thought. The insurance adjuster wouldn't offer Raina more money out of the kindness of her heart. "All the plates, platters, and utensils were donations. At most, they might have been worth fifty dollars. That's why I didn't include them in the claim. If you'd called, it would have saved you a trip."

"Is there a reason you don't want me here?" Alex asked.

Raina raised an eyebrow. Someone was on the defensive. "This place is an open book. We're not hiding anything here." She glanced at the cupboard. "We just want our legitimate claim processed so we can start rebuilding the heart of our community."

"We're still not done looking through the numbers."

"What can I do to help speed things along? I have provided price quotes for the repairs. I have filled out the required paperwork. I have even checked our claim against the policy, so I know I'm not asking for anything unreasonable. What else do you need?"

"These things take time. It is a large payout, and we have to dot every 'I' and cross every 'T'."

Raina narrowed her eyes. Something was wrong with this picture. She was done playing the nice quiet Chinese girl. Still holding the camera in front of her, she flipped open the cupboard door. There was an open can of paint thinner on the bottom shelf.

Alex's eyes widened, and she pointed an accusing finger at the paint thinner. "Ah-ha!" she exclaimed. "The accelerant for the fire. It was arson."

"I saw you put the can of paint thinner in the cabinet," Raina said. "You're looking for an excuse to deny the claim."

Alex stiffened, and she raised her chin. "I did no such thing." She whipped out her cell phone and took a picture of the cupboard. "The police report said the paper towels had an accelerant in them. And here it is. How do you explain this?"

Raina stared at the insurance adjuster in disbelief. She wasn't sure if her cell phone was zoomed in to show Alex placing the paint thinner in the cupboard. For all Raina knew, the video might not show anything useful at all, but Alex didn't know this. Raina should be angry, but she was more puzzled by the situation. This was a clumsy setup.

"I have been recording you from the second you stepped into the kitchen." Raina shook her phone. "Since the fire, we have also installed a motion sensor camera as well." She pointed to the far wall where her grandma had installed a white box the size of a walnut years ago. From a remote, the box would project ghosts onto the opposite wall for the center's haunted house. "The recording is in the basement."

Alex opened and closed her mouth. She blinked and opened her mouth again as if to say something but changed her mind again. She spun on her heels and marched out of the kitchen.

Raina trotted to keep up with the insurance adjuster. Maybe she didn't want to say something in front of the "camera" in the kitchen.

When it appeared that Alex might just walk out the front door, Raina called out, "If you don't talk to me, I will turn in the videos to your boss." Whatever Alex was up to, Raina didn't believe the entire insurance company approved of this behavior.

"Not until you turn off your phone," Alex said over her shoulder.

Raina turned off her cell phone and put it in her purse. "It's off."

Alex spun back around and crossed her arms. "I will put in the paperwork to approve your claim later today."

Raina should be shouting woohoo at the top of her lungs. She should be jumping for joy. She shouldn't spit at a gift horse. "Who put you up to this?"

Alex's eyes flickered. "I don't know what you're talking about."

"The senior center is a nonprofit. A politician might cut our budget, but even then, it has to be handled delicately because the retirees and their supporters can vote them out. Whatever you're up to, it has nothing to do with the senior center."

"I have another appointment. I need to get going."

Raina ran around Alex, blocking her exit. "So this means the claim denial is personal. We have never met before, so you have no personal reason to deny this claim. Which means someone put you up to it. Someone who doesn't like me."

"I don't have time for your conspiracy theory. I have to go." Alex brushed past Raina and ran out the door.

"It's not worth losing your job over this," Raina called out. "And when I find out who's behind this—"

The automatic doors swished shut.

Raina closed her mouth and fumed. How dare someone try to deny the fire claim for petty revenge? Who would do such a thing?

Her stomach rolled with guilt. Over the years, and through several murder investigations, she might have angered someone enough to jump at this opportunity to kill Raina's career at the senior center.

Wait! After such a confrontation, wouldn't Alex

reach out to the mastermind behind the scheme? She wouldn't dare put it in an email or text message because it would create a paper trail. She would probably meet with the culprit.

Raina ran into her office, grabbed her purse, locked the office door, and hung a sign that said she would be right back.

As Alex pulled out of the parking lot and onto the road, Raina hopped into her car. She pulled out, speeding up until she caught up with the silver Kia Sorrento.

Raina's heart thumped painfully, remembering the car accident from earlier in the day. Even though she doubted she was in anyone's crosshairs, she felt nervous. At every stop, she strained her ears, listening for any unusual sounds in her vehicle.

At the next stoplight, Raina ended up behind the silver Sorrento. She flipped the visor and straightened, hoping either the visor or the glare from the sun would hide her face.

In front of Raina, Alex moved the rearview mirror. Her eyes connected with Raina. The left turn lane changed from green to yellow.

Raina averted her gaze, breaking the eye contact. There was nothing fishy about her presence behind the insurance adjuster. This was a public road after all.

The silver Sorrento made a quick left turn just as the stoplight on the left lane changed to red. An oncoming car honked and slammed on the brakes to avoid a collision. The silver Sorrento disappeared from view.

12

OUT FOR BLOOD

Raina drove back to the senior center even more shaken than when she left it half an hour ago. The impromptu surveillance was a disaster. And it drove home the stakes in this murder investigation. Two people were dead. Father and son. Was Gabriel's death an accident or another murder?

And with Gabriel's death, the money passed on to the senior center. As the co-trustee with little oversight from Ms. Goldberg, Raina had free rein and access to the funds. If she were of a more devious nature, she could easily siphon the money for her personal use over the years with little chance of being caught. Once news of the trust became common knowledge, the police would view this as a motive for Raina to knock off the Escalante men, especially if there was something fishy about Gabriel's death. And no one would believe she didn't know about the bequest beforehand.

Raina parked and leaned her head on the steering wheel. She didn't want her husband to return home to find his wife arrested by his coworkers at the police station. How did a simple murder investigation turn so complicated?

And how did an insurance claim turn into a soap opera? Raina never imagined in her wildest dreams that the insurance adjuster would plant fake evidence to deny the claim. Or that someone probably pressured Alex into doing so. Was this Raina's arrogance coming back to roost? Had she stuck her nose one too many times into other people's business?

Sure, she had selfish reasons for investigating murders. It satisfied her curiosity and gave her a hobby to bond with her grandma. But didn't seeking justice for the dead balance out these selfish reasons? She was making a difference...right? Why would someone hold a grudge for this?

Raina's cell phone chirped. From the ringtone, she knew it was an incoming message from her grandma. She groaned out loud. What could it be now? Her grandma was babysitting little Gracie Sullivan. If this was an SOS over an exploding diaper, Raina was walking off into the sunset. She tapped on the message app.

COME QUICK! OUTSIDE JANICE'S CONDO. BIG PROBLEM!

"Are you kidding me?" Raina said. She didn't have time for this. Her grandma and Janice would have to duke it out. Raina didn't get paid enough to babysit naughty senior citizens. This wasn't part of her job description.

Her cell phone chirped again. This time the text was from Manny Díaz.

OUTSIDE JANICE'S CONDO. THERE WILL BE BLOOD!

Raina groaned out loud. She got out of the car and slammed it shut. It was one thing to ignore the message from her grandma, but it was an entirely different thing when Po Po disturbed other people. Raina stalked into the lobby of the condo complex and jabbed the call button for the elevator.

Her stomach heaved from the tension coursing through her body. While she didn't have the authority to force either woman to move out of the condo complex, she could ban their membership at the senior center. It was unprecedented, highly embarrassing for the parties involved, but it could be done. Po Po and Janice had forced Raina's hand.

The elevator doors dinged and slid open. Loud voices echoed down the hall. Raina stepped out of the elevator, cocked her head, and listened. She recognized both Po Po and Janice, but she wasn't familiar with the shrill voice. The male voice had to be Manny Díaz. So, four people were screaming at each other down the hall and around the corner, outside of Janice's condo. Great. Would she have to ban all four senior citizens?

Raina took a deep breath. Instead of jogging toward the conflict, she slowed her steps into a leisurely stroll. Better to see if the four retirees could straighten this argument out by themselves. Raina didn't want to get involved. And this would give her time to eavesdrop, so she didn't walk into the argument blind.

"...gold digger..."

"...his wife..."

"...divorced. You delusional, idiot," Po Po said.

Raina grinned. Her grandma sure didn't hold anything back. She made a great ally—except when she was against you—because she made an even greater enemy. Poor Janice.

"...leave, or I'll call the police," Janice said.

Raina picked up her pace. There was no need to get the cops involved. Then the Town Council might hear about this. She rounded the corner and gaped at the scene.

Po Po and Janice stood shoulder to shoulder, facing off Valerie Escalante and Manny Díaz. The two murder suspects had their backs to Raina and didn't notice her approach.

Raina held a finger to her lips. She didn't want Po Po and Janice to give away her presence. She tiptoed closer until the group was an arm's length in front of her. She had just crossed Manny off her suspect list, but now here he was again—with Valerie. What if the two of them were in cahoots together?

Po Po straightened, and her eyes gleamed with renewed vigor. The tension eased out of Janice's face, and she loosened her grip on the walker.

Raina felt a moment of shame for her earlier thoughts about these two women. In this moment of crisis, the two of them had come together on their own. Raina's chest swelled with pride. And she had the honor to be the custodian of this community.

"What's going on here?" Raina said sternly. "Manny, is this your guest?" Since Valerie did not live at the condo complex, she technically could not be on the private property without an escort.

Valerie spun around. When she saw that it was Raina by herself, she relaxed. "This doesn't concern you."

Raina raised an eyebrow. Valerie was technically right. Raina didn't have any authority over at the condo complex, but Janice did. She was part of the HOA. "Janice, maybe you should call the cops and give Manny a citation for breaking the HOA rules."

Manny held up both hands, palms out. "Whoa! This has nothing to do with me. I was passing through when I walked in on this. I am going back to my home now."

"Wait! Manny, you can't leave me here with these barbarians," Valerie said, her tone pleading.

"I don't want to get in trouble with the HOA. I love

living here," Manny said. He strolled down the hall, and his long legs carried him quickly out of view. Maybe he wasn't in cahoots with Valerie after all.

Valerie straightened and pointed a finger at Janice. "This person tricked Alonso into adding her name to his will. I will have my lawyer look into this. You are not getting one cent of the money."

Raina scratched her head. This argument was about Janice's bequest? "I don't get it. Even if Janice doesn't get the money, it's not like you will get the money."

Valerie shrugged. "It's the principle that counts. The money should go to my daughter. Alonso adopted her when she was a child. He had a financial responsibility toward Flora."

Raina gazed at Valerie for a long moment. Was the woman delusional or off her medication? First, she claimed to be still married to Alonso. And now this? "Flora is a grown woman. Alonso's financial responsibility toward your daughter ended years ago when she turned eighteen."

Valerie lifted her chin. "Which only shows that Alonso treated her like a daughter. She's entitled to an inheritance like Gabriel."

"Is this why you killed Alonso?" Raina asked. "You wanted Flora to inherit the money?"

"I didn't kill Alonso. I already told you, he was worth more to me alive than dead," Valerie said.

"Somebody saw you in the garden outside the

kitchen right before the fire," Raina said. "Did you lure him into the kitchen?"

Valerie rolled her eyes. "You are reading one too many detective novels, girlie."

"If you don't want to talk to me, you can always talk to the police," Raina continued, unperturbed with Valerie's rude behavior. "I'm sure you haven't told them about the garden. They would be interested to know you were near the scene of the crime."

Valerie's eyes shifted. She tucked her purse more firmly on her shoulder. "You will be hearing from my lawyer, you gold digger," she said to Janice. She started walking away.

Raina held out an arm, blocking Valerie. "I think Alonso's killer is knocking off his heirs. If I were you, I would be more afraid for your daughter's life. What's the use of getting a bigger share of the inheritance if she's dead?"

Valerie gave Raina a sharp look. "What are you talking about?" There was some hesitancy in her voice.

"Gabriel died from a car crash today," Raina said. "Isn't it mighty convenient that both father and son are dead? Who do you think will be next? You or Flora?"

Valerie paled. She blinked as if processing Raina's words. "Dead? How?"

"He wrapped his fancy new car around a tree," Raina said. Her voice sounded cold and distant. There was no sympathy for the woman in front of her, especially not after the way Valerie harassed poor Janice.

Valerie stumbled back and held out a hand to the wall for support. Raina took a step forward, holding out her hands.

Valerie waved her off. "I'm fine." She straightened, took a deep breath, and strode off. "You're wrong. No one is killing us off."

Once Valerie was out of the earshot, Po Po said, "I'm missing something here. We need tea and a chat."

Janice invited them into her home. But once inside, she made her slow way to her wingback chair and collapsed on it. Raina sat down on the loveseat.

Po Po hustled into the kitchen. Water ran from the faucet. A few seconds later, she popped her head out of the kitchen. "I put the kettle on. Where are the teabags, Janice?"

"In the drawer to the left of the stove," Janice called out. "Thanks, Bonnie."

For the next few minutes, they sat quietly in the living room while Po Po fixed tea in the kitchen. Once everyone had a steaming hot mug in front of them, Po Po sat down next to Raina in the loveseat.

Raina glanced at Janice. "Do you want to tell her about the bequest, or do you want me to tell the story?"

Janice gestured for Raina to go ahead. Raina told her grandma about Janice's bequest from Alonso, the car crash in front of the law office, and the trust for the senior center. Po Po's eyes grew wider and wider at each new reveal. When Raina was done with the story, everyone took a sip of the tea.

"As a trustee, you have a motive for getting rid of Gabriel," Po Po said.

"Not if she quits or gets fired," Janice said. "There's no guarantee she will hold this job forever. It seems like a big risk for a potential reward. Anyone with a brain wouldn't suspect Raina."

Po Po gave her arch nemesis a beaming smile. Anyone who appreciated her granddaughter got her grandma's approval. "What do we do now?"

Raina glanced from Po Po to Janice. Why were they looking at her for direction? "I'll get in touch with Detective Hopper and see if she can give us more information about the car crash."

"It's probably not an accident," Po Po said.

Raina nodded in agreement. That was her gut feeling as well. She hoped the murderer wasn't killing Alonso's beneficiaries off one by one. If this was the case, Janice and Raina would next be on the hit list. Yikes!

During the drive back home, Raina filled her grandma in on the incident in the kitchen with Alex and her lack of success in tailing the insurance adjuster.

"I can't believe I am saying this, but I need backup. Can the Posse Club help?" Raina said. She prayed she was doing the right thing. If the Town Council found out about this, she would be so fired.

Po Po gave her a salute. "I'm on it. We'll have a

special meeting at your house Sunday afternoon. Make sure to bake cookies."

Raina chuckled. "All right. Cookies and tea it is. It was sweet of you to support Janice. Valerie can be overwhelming."

"That didn't happen," Po Po said. "And if you tell anyone about it, I will deny it. Janice and I have a nice rivalry going on, and I want to keep it that way. I have a reputation to maintain. I'm the kooky one, and she's the stuffy one. Capeesh?"

"Oookay. No need to bust out the gangster slang," Raina said, suppressing the urge to roll her eyes. If her grandma wanted to maintain a fake rivalry with her arch nemesis, who was Raina to get in the way? She had more important things to worry about—like finding the killer before this person decided Raina was a threat.

13

DELUSIONS

The next morning, Raina grabbed two hot coffees and croissants from the Venus Café and strolled to Hook Park to the secluded gazebo by the pond. Mature trees hid the structure from the open grassy area of the park. It was the perfect hideaway for a tête-à-tête early in the morning, especially on the weekend. There would be no children cutting through the park on their way to school.

Detective Hopper sat on the wood bench, gazing at the ducks. Instead of her usual uptight French braid, her blonde hair was loose and flowing down her back. She wore jeans and a short-sleeve polo shirt. Without the officer uniform, the policewoman's cherubic face and baby blue eyes were more of a liability than an asset. And unlike Raina, Detective Hopper couldn't play the bimbolina to get answers from witnesses and suspects. The transition from officer to detective must have been difficult.

Raina sat down on the bench and handed over a coffee and a pastry bag. "Was Gabriel Escalante in a car crash yesterday?"

Detective Hopper gave Raina a sharp look. "We haven't released the identity of the driver yet. How did you get this information? Did Donna tell you this?"

Donna was the front desk clerk at the police station and Raina's source of information. "I was inside Goldberg and Associates when I heard the car crash." She swallowed the lump in her throat. "I recognized the red car. From the way the car was wrapped around the tree trunk, I assumed Gabriel didn't make it."

"They airlifted him to a hospital in Sacramento, but he died on the way there," Detective Hopper said.

They were silent for a long moment. Raina took a sip of coffee, gathering her thoughts. Under normal circumstances, she would have said this was a tragic accident. In a murder investigation, nothing was ever an accident.

"Was there something suspicious about the car crash?" Raina asked. She bit into the buttery croissant, and it melted in her mouth. Yum.

"Someone cut the brake line," Detective Hopper said and sipped the coffee.

The croissant settled into a cold lump in Raina's stomach. It must have been Flora. Who else would want Gabriel dead? She told the detective about the encounter outside the law firm and her suspicions. "Flora had time to cut the brake line. Gabriel, Janice, and I spoke for a while after she left."

"A few cross words don't automatically make someone a murderer. If that were the case, we would have a lot more dead bodies. Anything else to share?" Detective Hopper said, munching on the croissant.

Raina told Detective Hopper about her conversation with Manny Díaz, omitting the toilet explosion. There was no need for anyone ever to know Raina was covered from head to toe in gunk. She also spoke of the incident with Valerie outside of Janice's condo.

"Valerie sounds delusional to me. Why don't you suspect her of cutting the brake line?" Detective Hopper asked.

Raina shrugged. "She wasn't near the law firm?" The excuse sounded pretty lame.

"What if the mother and daughter were working together? Flora to distract you while Valerie cut the brake line."

"It's possible. What progress have you made on your inquiries?"

Detective Hopper crumbled the pastry bag into a ball and shot it into the trash can. "Your grandma turned on the burner on the stovetop right before the fire. Even your grandma doesn't remember if she turned it off."

"She turned it off. The fire was started after Alonso's death."

Detective Hopper held up both hands, palms out. "There's no need to be testy. I'm relating to you what I found out from talking to folks."

"And Janice Tally is my grandma's arch nemesis. Anything she says should be taken with a grain of salt."

Detective Hopper raised an eyebrow. "How did you know the story came from Janice?"

"She told me the same story. Do you think the two deaths are related? Father and son?" Raina asked. "Maybe money had nothing to do with it. Maybe the killings were acts of revenge."

Detective Hopper shrugged. "The only person who wanted revenge is Manny Díaz, and you ruled him out."

"What about Valerie? Maybe she has never forgiven Alonso for divorcing her."

"That's a little far-fetched. Valerie has remarried multiple times since the divorce. I don't think she's heartbroken about it at all. If she's the murderer, the motive has to be money. Or more money for her daughter."

"Then why did she keep his last name?"

Detective Hopper opened her mouth and promptly shut it. She thought for a second and said, "It's worth a shake. I'll stop by with the news about her stepson, and see what she has to say."

Raina squirmed. "I might have told her about Gabriel's car accident yesterday. I wanted to see how she would react."

Detective Hopper gave Raina a deadpan stare. "And how did she react?"

"She seemed shocked, and then she rushed off without a word. Maybe you can get something more out of her."

"What do you think will happen to Alonso's money now that Gabriel is dead?" Detective Hopper asked.

Raina considered her words carefully. If she told Detective Hopper about the trust for the senior center, it might derail the police investigation. After all, the policewoman would now have to expend energy to ruling out Raina as a potential murder suspect. And Raina wasn't in the mood to get into it.

"I think the lawyer has to see the death certificate and do paperwork before she can release the information," Raina said. Technically, she didn't lie to the police. She changed the subject. "I haven't heard a peep out of Officer Sokol since the day of the fire. I had expected him to harass us at the senior center."

"Strangely, he has been good. As in his usual lazy self, doing minimal work, sneaking off early, but at least he is not messing anything up or harassing anyone," Detective Hopper said. "I can't wait until Matthew comes back and takes Youri off my hands."

Raina thoughtfully sipped her coffee. While Officer Sokol's behavior might seem normal in all outward appearances, he wouldn't give up the chance to sabotage Detective Hopper's first case as lead detective. "Watch your back. He might just be biding his time."

"Trust me. I have one eye on him all the time. But his cousin is in town, so he has been preoccupied."

"Be thankful for small favors," Raina said. "Did you find out who was Alonso's last caller?"

"It's still being processed. Should show up any day now," Detective Hopper said.

Raina made a mental note to ask her grandma if her hacker had better luck with getting the phone number off Alonso's cell phone. As Raina walked home, she realized she had done most of the talking. Other than the cut brake line, Detective Hopper hadn't shared any other information about the investigation. Did this mean she was getting close to catching the murderer or that she didn't have a clue?

WHEN RAINA GOT HOME, Po Po was fixing matcha green tea in the kitchen. Her grandma whisked the green tea powder until it frothed. Raina told her grandma about the conversation with Detective Hopper at the park.

As Po Po buttered toast, she said, "Do you think the two deaths are linked?"

"They have to be linked," Raina said. "First, the father, and now the son. Will the killing stop now, or will it continue until the killer goes through everyone on the inheritance list?"

Po Po sipped her tea. "Why would this person kill all the beneficiaries? These murders are not random.

It's all targeted at the Escalante family. I think you and Janice are probably safe."

"Not unless the killer thinks I'm on the trail."

"Yeah, but this isn't something I want to think about," Po Po said slowly. She nibbled on her toast. "Who do you think is the murderer? Flora or Valerie?"

"I don't know. Maybe they are working together. Or maybe not. They were both seen near the senior center on the day of the fire. Flora was at the law firm, but she could have been a distraction while Valerie was fiddling with Gabriel's car. Even the housekeeper is a remote possibility."

"You don't think it's Janice?"

"No. Never even occurred to me. Though it was shocking to find out she was secretly dating Alonso."

Po Po chuckled. "Who knew Janice still had it going on."

"Now, don't you dare laugh at her. The poor woman was afraid you'd make fun of her. It's why she kept the relationship hidden."

"I'm more jealous than anything else. First, Maggie gets a man, and now Janice. I feel like the ugly stepsister." Po Po bit into her toast with more energy than before.

Raina gave Po Po a sly grin. "Manny Díaz seems to be interested in you. What do you think?" She wiggled her eyebrows suggestively.

Po Po choked on her toast. When she finished coughing, she gulped down the rest of her tea. "He's the type that will expect his woman to cook, clean, and cuddle." She paused for a moment. "Though the cuddling might be fun, it's not worth the headache. I'll need a backhoe to get rid of him."

Raina burst out laughing. "That bad, huh?"

Po Po nodded. "Not even remotely tempted. Anyway, I need to replace the carpet in my living room. The cleaning ladies did a good job, but I'm grossed out by the thought of touching the carpet with my bare feet."

Raina groaned. "I never want to talk about that evening again. I don't want anyone to know about this. I especially don't want Matthew thinking about it every time he kisses me. Is that understood?"

Po Po saluted at Raina. "Trust me. I don't want to think about it either. After your Uncle Anthony blew a gasket, he came through and dealt with the insurance and the neighbors. Back to the carpet—I say we go to Alonso's flooring shop and get Flora to help us."

"I like how your mind works. Can your hacker get into Alonso's cell phone? I still want to know who he was talking to before his death."

"The police don't have this information?"

Raina rolled her eyes. "It's the red tape. Detective Hopper seems to think she'll get the info soon, but I'm not holding my breath."

"I can call my hacker again. Maybe promise her a bonus." Po Po finished her toast. "Don't forget the Posse Club meeting is tomorrow. I promised the Lovebirds we'd have cookies. It's too bad we're missing Frank and Maggie. I left a message for Janice, but she hasn't called me back."

Raina raised an eyebrow. "Is Janice part of the club now?"

"No! This is a special one-time invite because we're short on people. I can't have her in the club. Half the time, we're plotting against her."

Raina burst out laughing again. At least her grandma was honest. "Let's roll."

14

NEW THREATS

The flooring shop was more like a warehouse. It took up an entire block next to the Bullseye store outside of town. Inside the automatic double doors, there were aisles and aisles of flooring samples, ranging from carpet to wood and even the cheaper linoleum. The overhead fluorescent lights beat down on the shoppers, and the neon orange sale signs screamed their discounts.

Raina had never seen so many flooring options in her life. When she had to put in new carpeting during the house remodel, her brother-in-law had given her a handful of possibilities within her price range. As Raina looked at all the options in front of her, she was thankful he helped narrow down her choices.

A saleswoman approached them with a wide smile. "What kind of flooring are we looking for today, ladies?"

"Is Flora Escalante available to help us?" Po Po asked.

The saleswoman stiffened. "She doesn't work on the weekends, but maybe I can help you. What are you looking for? Carpet or wood?"

"We're friends of the family. Her dad said that Flora would take care of us. Can you give me her phone number so I can call her?" Po Po asked.

The saleswoman's eyes widened, and the smile became fixed on her face like she was crept out but was too polite to show it. "We don't give out employees' phone numbers to random people. Flora will be here on Monday. You can come back then." She hurried toward a couple coming in through the front door without a backward glance.

"I feel abandoned. What kind of customer service is this?" Po Po said to no one in particular.

"Do you still want to look around?" Raina asked her grandma.

"No. I'll give Blue a call. He can narrow down the selection. I can't look through all the samples here. It'll give me a headache."

Raina wondered if her brother-in-law shouldn't open up a branch of his construction business in Sacramento. Between Raina and Po Po, Blue had driven back and forth from San Francisco more than a dozen times in the last year. And with the upcoming kitchen repair at the senior center, he would make even more trips.

"Let's go over to the mansion. Maybe Linda can help us find Flora," Raina said.

"Or maybe we can catch Valerie red-handed as she tries to sneak off with something from the mansion. Now I would love to call the police on her."

Raina chuckled. "That would be fun. But we need to have a conversation with Valerie. So far, each time we've seen her, she's been a pill."

"You mean a downright bit—"

"There's no need to spell it out, Po Po."

The drive to the mansion was uneventful, and they got there in twenty minutes. Unlike the neighboring mansions, Alonso's home didn't have a high wall or steel gate. Instead, a thick hedge wall lined the frontage. Raina pulled into the driveway and parked in front of the house.

Po Po pressed the doorbell, but once again, no one came to answer the door. Raina pulled out her cell phone and called the house. It rang and rang until an answering machine picked up. She called again and got the same result.

"I don't like this. No one is picking up," Raina said. "I'm going around the side to have a look-see. Do you want to stay here and keep trying the doorbell, or do you want to come with me?"

Po Po glanced around the circular driveway. "I'll come with you. I don't want to stand here by myself."

Raina suppressed the urge to shiver. There was something creepy about an empty mansion with just the butler, even though it was a housekeeper in this situation. The tall trees cast shadows on the circular driveway and provided a buffer from curious eyes and ears. If they screamed, would anyone hear them? She led them around the building to the garage.

The rollup doors were open, and parked in the rear of the tandem garage was an old Dodge Grand Caravan. The vehicle's sliding door and rear hatch were opened. The inside was stuffed with someone's earthly belongings in trash bags, plastic baskets, and cheap luggage. Someone was planning an escape.

Linda stepped out from the house with both arms around a red KitchenAid mixer. She stepped down to the garage carefully, peering around the load in her arms. When she saw Raina and Po Po next to the van, she froze. Her gray blonde hair was in a bun on the top of her head. Strands of hair floated around her angular face, but it did nothing to soften her determined expression. After a moment of hesitation, she marched over and shoved the mixer onto the floor of the passenger seat.

She stepped back and leaned against the van, blocking the inside with her body. "What are you doing here?" Her posture was stiff, and the smile held no warmth.

Raina wondered if all the items in the van actually belonged to the housekeeper. "Where are you going, Linda? You said it would take a shovel to get you to leave this cushy job."

Linda's smile wavered. After half a second, she gave up the attempt. "Gabriel is dead. I'm not sitting in this empty house, waiting for the killer to come for me."

"What about arranging Alonso's funeral?"

Linda averted her gaze. "The lawyer will have to take care of it. As it is, I'm not even sure I will get my last paycheck. And my life is worth more to me than money."

From the corner of Raina's eye, she saw Po Po edging around the van to go toward the doorway to the kitchen. She wanted to scream for her grandma to stop. Who knew what lurked inside? But if she did, Linda would clam up. She prayed her ancestors would take care of her grandma.

"Why would the murderer want to kill you?" Raina asked. "Wouldn't this person go after Valerie or Flora? It seems to me like someone wants to wipe out the Escalante family."

"Those two are Escalante in name only. They probably took his name, hoping to get some of the money."

"You don't think Alonso left them some money? I saw Flora outside the law firm on the day Gabriel died."

"She's not in the will. If she was there, the lawyer probably wanted her to provide oversight on the business for Gabriel. He was more of a child than a grown man, if you know what I mean."

Raina thought about how Gabriel and Flora bickered and got on each other's nerves outside the law firm. Was there a sibling rivalry between the two? Gabriel had denied that Flora was a sibling, but did she feel the same way? She was still family, whether or not he wanted it.

"Why would she help Gabriel? Especially since he wanted nothing to do with her," Raina asked.

Linda shrugged. "You'll have to ask her. The money is probably cursed."

Raina suppressed the urge to shiver. She didn't believe in curses, but she had a healthy respect for them. In Chinese culture, curses and luck were different sides of the same coin. "Where are you going? How will the lawyer get you the money? I thought you were planning to purchase a condo."

Linda slammed the passenger door shut and pressed the button to close the sliding door and the rear hatch. "She can mail the check to my sister's house. I plan to disappear until this whole thing blows over."

It wasn't lost on Raina that Linda still planned to keep the money, even though it might be cursed. "If you disappear like this, people will think you're the killer."

"I don't care what anyone thinks. The police will catch the culprit."

"Maybe. Maybe not. There's a reason we have all these cold cases and unsolved mysteries. Didn't the police tell you not to leave town? They won't be happy if you disappear," Raina said, wondering if she should call Detective Hopper.

Linda turned to the van and dug around inside. When she turned back to Raina, there was a garage remote in her hand. "I'm not a suspect." She pulled a key from the pocket of her jeans and held out the remote and key.

Raina took the items. "Are they for the mansion?"

Linda nodded. "Can you please turn them over to Ms. Goldberg? I don't want to spend another night in this house. If you don't want to help, then I'll hide them under a rock and tell her about the hiding spot over the phone."

Raina's hand curled over the remote and key. There was no way she was giving them up. She could snoop to her heart's content after this conversation. "I'll take care of it for you."

"Thanks a lot. You might want to tell your friend to keep a low profile. She might be on the killer's hit list too."

It took Raina a moment to recall that she had told Linda in a previous conversation about Janice inheriting some of Alonso's money. "It won't come to that."

Linda hopped into the van and turned on the engine and headlights. She rolled down a window and called out, "Take care."

As Raina watched the van leave the driveway, she pulled out her cell phone and dialed Detective Hopper's number. It went to voicemail.

Raina left a message about Linda skipping town. Now the ball was in the detective's court.

She strolled to the house, calling out, "Po Po! Where are you?"

There was no answer.

Raina pulled out her cell phone and called her grandma. It went to voicemail. She left her grandma a message to let her know that Linda had left and to return to the kitchen. She texted her grandma the same message.

As much as Raina would like to explore the mansion, it would be better to do it together so they could keep track of each other. Linda probably didn't get around to changing the locks, so Flora and Valerie might both still have access to the house. And since the two of them were on the top of the suspects list, Raina didn't want her grandma or herself to confront either of them alone.

Raina's cell phone rang, and she tapped on the app to accept the call. "Po Po, where are you?"

"Upstairs in the south wing. Second door on the left," her grandma said.

"Are you wearing gloves? You don't want to leave behind fingerprints," Raina said.

"Oops. Too late now, huh?"

Raina groaned. "Come back to the kitchen. We can go out to my car to get gloves."

Through the phone, it sounded like Po Po was

walking in the hallway. "What is a nice girl like you doing with gloves in your car?"

"I have a police detective for a husband. Sometimes he uses my car." Raina had an entire police kit in her trunk, but she didn't dare tell Po Po this. Her grandma might want to play with it.

Po Po laughed. "Uh-huh. I wonder how many murderers have used this excuse."

Her grandma marched into the kitchen a few seconds later. They walked through the house to the front door. Raina opened it, and they strolled up to her car in the circular driveway.

Raina popped the trunk and stuck her head inside, pulling out the black duffel bag. "Linda also gave me the key and garage remote for the house. If we don't finish today, we can always come back tomorrow."

Po Po stepped around the car. "Rainy, there is something on your windshield." Her voice sounded concern.

Raina pulled out the gloves and several plastic Ziploc sandwich bags. While she wasn't planning to remove anything from the house, if she found something interesting she might borrow it for closer examination. She slammed the trunk closed. "What did you say?"

"It looks like someone stuck a letter on your windshield."

Raina walked around the car and stood next to her grandma. Sure enough, there was an envelope stuck to her windshield. She reached for it, but Po Po swatted at her hand.

"Put on your gloves. We might need to get prints off of it," Po Po said.

Raina put on the latex gloves and handed a pair to her grandma. "Good thinking."

She reached for the envelope and held it up into the late afternoon sunlight. There was no writing on it. Very odd. "Should I open it? Or wait until later?"

"Open it. It's probably a threatening letter from the killer. It's some variation of 'stop investigating or else.' These types of letters are never original," Po Po said.

Her grandma was trying to lighten the mood, so Raina smiled. A knot settled into her chest. It didn't matter how many times she had gotten threatening letters. Each time, it still made her skin crawl all the same. She opened the flap and peered inside. The paper was a fancy thick linen stock. She couldn't make out any words.

"What's inside? A strand of hair? A finger?" Po Po asked, trying to peer over Raina's shoulders.

"A blank letter."

"What?"

Raina pulled out the folded sheet. A fine white powder floated up around her. She dropped the paper and backed up, dragging her grandma with her.

"What's that?" Po Po asked.

The powder drifted to the ground, settling like white spores on the asphalt.

"I don't know. Did you breathe any of it in?" Raina asked.

"I don't know. Did you?" Po Po asked, sounding worried.

Raina swallowed. Her throat didn't feel tight. Her nostrils weren't burning. "I probably didn't. Is it Anthrax?"

15

DEAR FRENEMY

They both took several steps back. Raina took off her gloves, flipping them inside out to contain the residual powder. She pulled out a plastic sandwich bag and put the gloves inside, zipping the opening closed.

"I better called the police," Raina said. She was proud that her voice didn't tremble.

"That letter will fly away with the next breeze. I'll drop a rock on top of it." Po Po looked in the mulch next to the front steps.

"Throw the rock. I don't want you close to that powder again," Raina said, dialing nine-one-one. She spoke to dispatch and explained the situation. She hung up and turned to her grandma. "Someone is coming."

They sat at the top of the steps and waited. A

handful of mulch held down the envelope and sheet of paper, the ends fluttering in the breeze.

"Maybe we should cover it up. The wind might blow the powder away," Po Po said.

"There is probably enough inside the envelope for testing," Raina said. "I don't want to go anywhere near that stuff. We don't know what it is."

"Who do you think put the letter on your windshield? The housekeeper?" Po Po asked.

Raina shook her head. "I watched Linda drive away. She would have to turn around to come back up the driveway."

"How hard is it to turn around? She wouldn't even break a sweat," Po Po said.

Raina nodded to appease her grandma, not in agreement. "Did Linda strip the house?"

Po Po shook her head. "There are a few missing items from the kitchen. Probably enough to set up her place. Which kind of makes sense, considering that she lived here for the last fifteen years. She probably doesn't have any utensils."

"Anything else?"

"A few paintings are gone. You can tell from the faded wallpaper where the paintings were once mounted. Two big-screen TVs are missing. A few objects in the sitting rooms. Yes, they have multiple ones. The maid service didn't do a good job. You can tell from the dust that knick knacks have been removed. Assuming they were of the same caliber as the ones left behind, they were expensive knickknacks. But I didn't see them in Linda's van. She could have dropped off a load before we caught her."

Raina mulled over her interaction with Linda. She shook her head. "It's probably not Linda. She thinks the killer is going after the heirs one by one. Since Alonso's death, she had plenty of opportunities to rob the mansion, but she didn't. And don't forget, things were disappearing before today."

Her gaze drifted back to the letter on the circular driveway, and she suppressed the urge to shiver. The killer knew Raina was investigating the deaths. And this person might have been inside the mansion with her grandma.

A police cruiser pulled up behind Raina's Honda Accord. Officer Sokol got out and slammed the door. His pug face scowled at Raina and Po Po. "What's this about a poisoned letter?"

Raina stood up stiffly from the front steps and made her way to her car. "An anonymous note on my car. When I opened the envelope, white powder came out. It might be anthrax."

Officer Sokol sighed. "Just make enemies wherever you go, don't you?"

Raina bit her tongue. She refused to sink to his level. He was looking for an excuse to dismiss her concern.

Officer Sokol waited for Raina's reply. When it wasn't forthcoming, he turned his attention to the paper on the ground. "I got to call out the hazmat team. Sit tight." He returned to the police cruiser and radioed in his request.

Raina returned to her grandma. "He's in a mood."

"So am I," Po Po said, crossing her arms. "If that man doesn't watch his manners, I'm filing a complaint."

Officer Sokol returned to grill them. His questions implied this was a hoax, but he was a good guy for following the protocol to get the powder tested. Raina and Po Po answered his questions as patiently and calmly as they could. When the hazmat team took away the threatening letter, Officer Sokol left with them.

Raina locked the front door and closed the garage doors. If the killer was still inside the mansion, she didn't care. She wasn't going anywhere near this house again until she got over the heebee jeebees.

They picked up a pizza for dinner. Po Po was in a grumpy mood, and Raina didn't blame her. They went through the motion of eating and spent the rest of the evening watching TV until they could call it an early night.

The next morning, Raina woke early for a run. She came home, showered, and baked cookies and a coffee cake for the meeting later in the afternoon. Po Po didn't come down from the guest room until lunchtime.

Po Po sniffed the air and beamed. "This smells real good. I'm glad we'll have a nice quiet afternoon for a change. I'm not sure how much more of this excitement I can take."

Raina suppressed the urge to snort. Her grandma didn't do quiet. She slid plates of egg and cheese bagel sandwiches onto the kitchen island. "What do you want to drink?" She had made an iced coffee for herself.

"Milk oolong?" Po Po asked, yawning. She pulled out a barstool and sat on the other side of the kitchen island.

Raina pulled out a terra-cotta teapot and cup. She poured boiling water into the teapot to warm it up. A few seconds later, she poured the water into the sink. She put in a scoop of the loose leaf tea, poured boiling water over it, and slid the teapot and cup to her grandma. She walked around the kitchen island and pulled out the barstool to join her grandma.

They ate quietly for several long minutes. With the kitchen window open, Raina heard birds chirping in the backyard. A dog barked in the distance, and a car door slammed shut—normal Sunday midday sounds. The threatening letter from the night before almost felt like it had happened to someone else.

Raina shuddered at the thought of her grandma touching the white powder. The killer was on to them now. Was it time to stop the investigation?

"What are you thinking about?" Po Po asked, wiping her mouth with a napkin.

"I'm asking myself if we should stop the investigation. I don't want either of us to get hurt," Raina said. She took a long sip of her ice coffee.

"It was nasty business last night, but the show must go on," Po Po said. "Alonso was a friend and benefactor to the senior center. With the money he left the center, we would be financially solvent for years to come. We have to solve the case. It's the right thing to do."

Raina sighed. Her grandma was right, but it didn't make the threat any less dangerous. "I'm starting to doubt my ability to carry on this investigation. Everything at the senior center is a mess. The budget is blown out of the water from ordering takeout for the hot meal program. We can't use the facility because of the smoke and fire damage. Each day we go on like this, the more I worry about getting fired. I didn't realize how much I love this job until now."

"Did Alex send over the approval for the claim?" Po Po asked.

"No, she didn't. Maybe she didn't have enough time to get it in on Friday afternoon. But if the approval doesn't come in by tomorrow afternoon, I am calling the insurance company to ask for a new insurance adjuster."

"It might not be a good idea. A new adjuster might take even longer because this person would go back to square one."

"Then I guess we're stuck with Alex Kovac," Raina said reluctantly. She had reviewed the video recording on her phone. It showed Alex's hand going into the cupboard. Unfortunately, the video clip was blurry, so Raina couldn't tell if Alex's hand was empty or holding the paint thinner. If push came to shove, Raina had no evidence of any wrongdoing.

"Don't worry. The Posse Club has your back. I sent out an SOS to all our contacts yesterday, asking for information on Alex Kovac. We will know more when we have our meeting this afternoon."

WHEN PO PO went upstairs to check her email and social media, the doorbell rang. Raina glanced at the goldfish clock with gilded kois swimming around the dial. It was only half past twelve. Much too early for the Posse Club meeting.

Raina looked through the peephole in her front door.

Detective Hopper stood on the porch, tapping her foot. She wore a blouse and jeans, but her blonde hair was in a tight French braid, and her blue eyes flashed daggers. Something had got Detective Hopper riled up, and Raina wasn't sure if she wanted to be the recipient of the policewoman's anger.

"I know you're in there, Raina. I can see your car in the driveway," Detective Hopper yelled.

Raina backed away from the peephole. Great. The anger was directed at her. The cell phone in her back pocket rang.

"I can hear your phone ringing," Detective Hopper called out.

Raina took a deep breath, plastered on a broad smile, and opened the front door. She gestured for the policewoman to come in.

Detective hopper stalked in, her braid swishing behind her back. "I just found out that you are getting Alonso's money."

Raina shook her head. "The senior center is getting Alonso's money. The director is a co-trustee. It just so happens that I fill this position for now."

"Which will be plenty of time for you to siphon off the money."

Raina stiffened at the insult. "What are you accusing me of?"

"Why didn't you tell me about the trust yesterday?" Detective Hopper asked.

"How did you hear about it?" asked Raina. Surely the lawyer wasn't disclosing this information to everyone.

"I heard about it at the Venus Café. Apparently, I was the only person who didn't know about it."

Butterflies settled in Raina's stomach. How did the rumor mill work so quickly? "I found out on the day Gabriel died. It seemed disrespectful to ask the lawyer for the details until later."

Detective Hopper narrowed her eyes. "How can I trust you after this? It's just like you to withhold information."

Raina bristled at the tone. "You're unbelievably rude. I've shared everything I found out in this investigation. And yet, you keep your cards close to your chest."

"I can't trade information with you like we're in a sleepover party. I'll lose my job or get reprimanded for leaking information about an ongoing investigation."

Raina suppressed the urge to roll her eyes. If the policewoman was concerned about her job, she shouldn't have proposed they partner up in the first place. The last comment was thrown in to make Raina feel guilty for expecting tit-for-tat. "I don't understand why you're upset."

Detective Hopper took a step forward, closing in on Raina's personal space. Through gritted teeth, she said, "This makes you a suspect."

Raina shrugged with a nonchalance she didn't feel. "I've been a suspect before. I don't see why it's a big deal. You and I both know I didn't kill Alonso or Gabriel."

Detective Hopper crossed her arms. "Actually, I don't know this."

Raina took a deep breath. "You've got to be kidding. I am married to a homicide detective. And we have known each other for years. Do you think I am capable of killing anyone?"

"Everyone is capable of murder, given the right circumstances. And you are no exception. And for your information, I know how much this house and the remodel cost you and Matthew. For all I know, you could be in a deep financial hole."

Raina let out a nervous laugh and stifled it midstream. Between the reward money for finding the murderer for Phil Lutz's brother and the loan from Po Po, the remodel came in on budget. And in the intervening months, they had slowly rebuilt their savings account. The financial details of their household were none of the policewoman's business.

"Besides our mortgage, Matthew and I have no debt," Raina said. "Both of us drive cars that are over ten years old."

Detective Hopper rolled her eyes. "You don't need to pretend. Everyone has debt. And even if you don't, it never hurts to have more money."

Raina didn't want this conversation to get sidetracked by the trust for the senior center. "I got a threatening letter yesterday. The killer must have somehow found out that I am investigating the deaths."

"So I've heard from Youri. But how do I know you didn't plant the letter yourself?"

Raina suppressed her rising irritation. First, Office Sokol said the letter was a hoax, and now Detective Hopper thought Raina planted it. "Why would I do this?"

"To throw us off the trail," Detective Hopper said, shrugging. "To get attention."

"This is unbelievable," Raina said, not bothering to

hide her anger. "You're unbelievable." She opened the front door. "It's time for you to leave."

As Detective Hopper stepped through, she said, "Stay out of my investigation. I would hate to charge you with obstruction."

16

OPERATION HUMBLE PIE

A few hours later at the Posse Club meeting, Raina's anger had simmered down to annoyance at Detective Hopper's parting comment. There was no point in dwelling on it. She passed out mugs of hot tea and set the tray against the wall of her dining room. Maybe she should purchase a sideboard before her next dinner party.

Raina joined the retirees at the dining room table and glanced around at the familiar faces. Warmth filled her heart. The Posse Club members talked among themselves and munched on cookies.

The Lovebirds were one of those rare couples in the senior community who had been together for over fifty years. The husband was an ex-air force pilot, and his Korean wife used to be a nurse. They held hands under the table.

Manny Díaz nibbled on a cookie, breaking off

small pieces on his napkin. The breeze from the overhead ceiling fan lifted his dull white hair. His deep brown eyes were wary as if waiting for someone to kick him from the room.

Po Po rapped at the table, and the conversation died down. She wore her pink combat fatigues. It was her grandma's outfit for reconnaissance meetings before an operation. Her laptop was on the table in front of her, along with a white box.

"Thank you for volunteering to be part of Operation Humble Pie," Po Po said. She gestured at Manny. "We have a new recruit. Welcome, Manny."

The Lovebirds clapped.

Raina joined them. She was surprised they didn't have the newbie do an initiation stunt worthy of the rowdiest fraternity. "I'm surprised you didn't invite Janice Tally."

"I called her," said Mrs. Lovebird. "But it went straight to voicemail. I left her a message, but she probably didn't get it in time."

"The call to Janice was a one-time offer since we are missing a couple of our regular members," Po Po said. She glanced around the table. "We are not opening the membership to my arch nemesis."

"Of course not," Mrs. Lovebird murmured.

"We wouldn't dream of it," Mr. Lovebird said.

Manny just grinned.

"Rainy, can you turn off the lights?" Po Po asked.

Raina flicked the switch, wondering why they

were sitting in the dark. There was enough ambient light coming in from the kitchen and dining room to make out everyone's face even without the overhead lights.

Po Po clicked the button on the white box. It whirled, and a light came on. It was the smallest projector that Raina had ever seen. Po Po tapped on the laptop, and a photo of Alex Kovac filled the wall in front of them.

"This is Alex Kovac, the insurance adjuster, and public enemy number one to the senior center," Po Po said. She filled the group in on the status of the claim so far.

"Is Operation Humble Pie to get Alex to approve the insurance claim?" Manny asked.

"Yes, and to find out who put her up to sabotaging it," Raina said.

"I forwarded her photo to my contacts earlier," Mrs. Lovebird said. "She's staying at the Fireside Motel."

Raina didn't know Alex was from out of town. The insurance company was based out in the Midwest, but Raina figured they had someone local to take care of the claims. Alex's car had a California plate, but it might be a rental.

"We'll start our surveillance there tomorrow," Po Po said. "We need to know who she talks to and her daily routine."

"We can split into teams of two. Raina can run HQ," Mr. Lovebird said.

"Does that mean we're partnering up, Bonnie?" Manny asked, his eyes gleaming.

Po Po gave him a deadpan stare. "Yes, but don't get too excited. I am not a morning person."

"And I love a challenge," he said.

The Lovebirds shared a knowing look.

Raina raised her hand. "What's HQ?"

"The senior center, my dear," Mrs. Lovebird said. "You have to work, but you can bring the walkie talkie into the office with you."

While the senior citizens hashed out the details for the surveillance, Raina munched on another cookie. Hopefully, she would find out who was behind the scheme to deny the senior center's insurance claim.

BY SEVEN IN THE MORNING, the senior citizens were already in position at the Fireside Motel parking lot. If the insurance adjuster had to leave early in the morning, the Posse Club didn't want to miss her.

Raina dragged herself to work with her travel mug of coffee. Her grandma had made her breakfast, a peanut butter and jelly sandwich. She powered up her computer, stifling a yawn.

With a walkie talkie by her side, she spent the next hour finishing up the budget for the Town Council. She wrote a memo detailing the cuts to their existing programs. Until the trust from Alonso came through, she couldn't count on the money for the next fiscal year's budget.

As she finished the last bite of the PB&J sandwich, the walkie talkie crackled to life.

"Humble Pie is on the move," Po Po said through the airwaves.

Raina pressed the button on the walkie talkie. "Be careful, everyone. Don't get into a car accident. If you lose Alex, we can try again tomorrow."

"Ten-four," Mrs. Lovebird said.

"This is the most fun I had all month," Manny said.

Raina got up from her desk and went to use the restroom. After she did her business, she walked over to the Venus Café to stretch her legs and get another coffee. When she returned to her office twenty minutes later, there was an email from the claim adjuster.

As she clicked on the email, her heartbeat kicked up a notch in anticipation. It popped open on her screen. Claim approved.

Raina did a fist pump and yelled, "Woohoo!" She got up from the desk and did a happy dance.

She grabbed the walkie talkie and clicked on the button. "Humble Pie just sent over the approval for the claim. Where was she twenty minutes ago?"

"At the coffee shop with her laptop. We went in and got pastries too, but she didn't even glance our way," Mr. Lovebird said.

"When you're old, you're practically invisible," Mrs. Lovebird said.

"Keep up the good work," Raina said. "Signing off. I've got to call the contractor."

Raina hung up and called her brother-in-law. They made arrangements for construction to start at the end of the week.

In the foyer, the student interns were setting up the table for the hot meal distribution. Once again, the rec room was booked for the rest of the week.

Raina strolled out of her office. "We finally got the approval for the insurance claim. We're getting a new kitchen."

The two students cheered and high-fived each other. One of them called out, "I can't wait until we get our regular hours back."

"Me too," Raina said. Without needing meal preparation, she had to reduce the interns' hours. It was either that or furlough half of them.

She mentally went through her to-do list. It was time to check on Janice. She grabbed a bag lunch. "I'll deliver this to Janice Tally."

Raina strode to the elevator and pushed the call button. She hadn't seen or heard from Janice since the awful confrontation with Valerie. The elevator came, and Raina got inside.

A few minutes later, she was outside of Janice's condo unit. Raina pressed the doorbell. No answer. She knocked and peered into the peephole. Still no answer.

Raina frowned. Janice was a regular at the hot meal

program. During the last years of Janice's husband's life, the nursing care for him had depleted most of her savings. She relied on the free meal to stretch her tight budget. Unless she was out of town, the retiree didn't miss lunch.

Pressing her ear to the door, Raina dialed Janice's home phone number. A phone rang inside. It rang until the answering machine came on.

"Hi, Janice. It's Raina. I got your lunch bag. I'm outside your front door."

Raina hung up and glanced at the door, expecting it to open. When nothing happened, she called Janice again. The answering machine picked up.

"I'm taking your meal back downstairs," Raina said. "Come by and grab lunch. Give me a call, so I know you're okay."

There was a short line for the meal distribution in the foyer. Raina handed the bag lunch to the student intern and returned to her office, deep in thought.

Something about the current situation didn't sit right. Mrs. Lovebird had left a message a few days ago to invite Janice to the Posse Club meeting. She didn't get a response. And today, Janice wasn't in her home or downstairs to grab a lunch. The retiree didn't own a cell phone or a car. She wouldn't have left town without a word.

Raina sent a group text to several of Janice's cronies.

DID ANYONE SEE JANICE THIS WEEKEND? SHE DIDN'T
STOP BY FOR LUNCH TODAY.

Within seconds, she got several text messages back. All of them said they hadn't seen Janice since Friday.

Raina frowned at the messages. Now, this was troubling. It had been more than forty-eight hours since anyone laid eyes on the retiree. Was it too early to sound the alarm?

She replied to the group text.

ANYONE WITH A SPARE KEY TO JANICE'S CONDO? AND
CAN YOU CHECK HER UNIT? I WANT TO MAKE SURE SHE
DIDN'T FALL DOWN IN HER HOME.

A silent shudder probably went through the entire group. No one feared a fall more than senior citizens.

A few minutes later, Raina got a reply.

NO JANICE IN HER CONDO.

Raina wanted to ask if there were signs of a struggle, but it might be too much for Janice's friends. According to Linda William, the killer was getting rid of Alonso's heirs one by one. Did this person lure Janice out from the safety of her home?

Raina pushed the unease aside. Janice was a grown woman. She knew how to take care of herself. Raina was probably jumping at shadows because of the threatening letter. She picked up the walkie talkie and pressed the talk button.

"Sunshine here. Have we made any progress with Humble Pie? The approval for the claim came in," Raina said.

The walkie talkie crackled to life. "Humble Pie is having lunch in Hook Park with..." Po Po's voice got cut off by static.

Raina pressed the talk button again. "Who is she having lunch with?"

Mrs. Lovebird's voice crackled through the airwaves. "She's with..."

Raina frowned at the static. The range on the walkie talkies shouldn't be a problem. Maybe there was interference from overhead power lines.

She got up and grabbed her purse. Hook Park was just around the corner. She needed a walk and a distraction from her thoughts. Maybe she could catch Alex meeting with the mastermind.

17

THE LAST CALLER

Raina made a beeline for the secluded gazebo by the pond. With mature trees hiding the structure from the grassy area and the playground, it was the perfect location for a nefarious meeting.

By the time she got to the park parking lot, she was slightly out of breath. From here, a dirt path led to the back of the gazebo. Most visitors would be too busy looking at the ducks on the pond to pay attention to someone approaching from behind.

Raina should be able to sneak up on Alex. The wild card was the Posse Club. Were they hiding in plain sight by pretending to be visitors at the park? Or pretending to be spies and hiding among the trees and shrubs? Either scenario could blow Raina's cover if she wasn't careful.

Raina crouched down and tiptoed forward, going

into stealth mode. Her senses appeared to be on hyperdrive. Birds trilled overhead, and squirrels chattered at each other. Her nose itched at the fragrant white dogwood and cherry trees blooming among the oaks. Did she take her allergy medicine today? The tree branches crackled underneath her feet. So much for stealth mode.

As she crept through the line of trees, she saw two people sitting on the bench in the gazebo. They were facing the pond with their backs to Raina. The sun was in front of them, so Raina could only make out shadowy figures. Judging from the shape of their bodies and hairstyles, Alex's companion was a man. A short man.

Two more trees stood between Raina and the edge of the gazebo. She was still too far away to hear the conversation. Through the canopy of trees, the walking path that encircled Mildred's Pond appeared to be empty. Where were the Posse Club members?

Raina took a deep breath, her heart pounding in anticipation. This was it. She would find out who wanted to deny the insurance claim. She glided to the first tree. After several seconds, she peered out from behind the tree. Alex and her companion were still on the bench, facing the pond.

Raina stepped out from the protection of the tree, took two steps, and froze. Her jaw dropped, and she blinked several times.

Po Po sprang out from the tree to the right of the

gazebo, brandishing her cell phone and crackling with amusement. From the way she held it in front of her, she appeared to be recording Alex and her companion.

From the left of the gazebo, Mrs. Lovebird sprang out from behind the hedge, also waving her cell phone in one hand while talking into the walkie talkie with the other. The cell phone was facing the wrong way.

The man jerked up, holding his hands in front of his face. He spun on his heels, jumped off the gazebo platform, and dashed off. For a short man, he was quick on his feet.

Twigs crackled and shrubbery rustled. Footsteps pounded after the man. Mr. Lovebird and Manny must be chasing after the culprit.

Raina stomped into the gazebo. "Well, well, well. It's my favorite insurance adjuster."

Alex whirled around. Her startled expression might have been comedic if it weren't for the serious nature of the situation. She froze for half a heartbeat and thawed to clutch her purse in front of her. Her pencil skirt and kitten heels weren't made for a quick getaway. She was a sitting duck.

Po Po and Mrs. Lovebird slinked off on the path around the pond.

"I've emailed you the claim approval," Alex said.

"Thank you. I have already gotten in touch with the contractor. He will start later in the week," Raina said.

Alex nodded. "Good. Now if you will excuse me." She took a step back.

"Not so fast," Raina said. Her voice was tight. She took a deep breath to calm down. "What are you doing with Youri Sokol?"

Alex blinked several times. "I don't know who you are talking about."

Raina took a step closer and jerked her thumb in the direction of the chase. "The man that ran off. That's Youri Sokol. Short, stout, and pug face."

Several expressions flickered across Alex's face. Finally, she threw up her hands. "It's not a crime to meet a friend at a park."

Raina cocked her head. Detective Hopper had mentioned that Officer Sokol had been busy with a family member in town. "I think he's more than a friend. He's your cousin."

Alex opened and closed her mouth. "What do you want from me? You already got your claim approval."

Raina took another step forward until she was within Alex's personal space. "Consider this your warning. Never pull another stunt like this. Now get out of here before I change my mind."

"What will you do to my cousin?"

Raina gave her a grim smile. "I'll think of something."

Alex hurried off without a backward glance.

Raina stepped off the gazebo and onto the walking path. She glanced around but didn't see Po Po or Mrs. Lovebird. The retirees must have gone back to HQ.

She took a deep breath, feeling the tension leave

her. At least now she knew who was working against her. It was the low-down rat, Youri Sokol. She wasn't naïve. He would probably try to undermine her again, but at least it wouldn't put her job in jeopardy.

And without proof, there wasn't much she could do anyway. All she had was a blurry video clip of Alex reaching into the cupboard at the senior center. And if Po Po got a video clip—which Raina doubted—it would show Alex sitting next to Youri on a park bench. This was not sufficient evidence for the police chief to reprimand Youri.

Busting in on this secret meeting would probably keep Youri in line for a while. Like all rats, he avoided direct confrontation, preferring to scurry in the shadows. And once Raina's husband found out about this scheme, he would probably make life miserable for Officer Sokol. In the future, the officer might run the other direction when he saw her coming.

RAINA STOPPED BY THE EATERY, the cafeteria-style dining hall in the middle of the university. The student-friendly pricing and the free parking made the Eatery a popular place for locals to grab a cheap lunch. Since it was close to two o'clock, there were no lines.

She ordered a Mucho Steak Burrito from the Mexican station and an iced hazelnut latte from Java Java. She deserved a treat for catching Sokol red-handed, or at least that would be the story she told her husband later on. She snickered to herself at the thought. She was turning out to be just as bad as her grandma.

Raina strolled back to the senior center with a full stomach and half a burrito for lunch tomorrow. Life was looking good at the moment. When she unlocked her office door, she found Po Po with her feet up on the desk and munching from the box of chocolate truffles Raina kept hidden in the filing cabinet.

Raina frowned at her grandma. "How did you get in here? And how did you find my chocolates?"

Po Po swung her feet down to the ground and sat up in the swivel chair. "My nose knows. I can always smell good chocolate."

"Don't distract me with your nose." Raina held out her hand, wiggling her fingers. "Give me the copy of the key."

"Are you sure you want it back? What if you lock yourself out someday?"

"I can always call the facilities person at Town Hall."

Po Po pulled out a key from her beach bag-sized purse. She dangled it over Raina's palm, reluctant to let it go. "But then you have to wait until the person they send gets here. Wouldn't it be better to have a spare key here with someone you trust?"

Raina curled her hand around the key. "I'll take my chances. And you better leave me the last piece in the box. If I can't get my emergency chocolate when I'm having a bad day, I know where you live."

Po Po put the lid back on the box. "And this is the thanks I get for helping you crack the Case of the Shady Insurance Adjuster."

Raina burst out laughing at her grandma's theatrics. "Is that what we're calling it now?" She put away her purse and the box of chocolates.

Po Po got up to give Raina back her chair.

"I'm heading to the kitchen," Raina said. "I need to check the cupboards and refrigerators. I can have the interns pack up anything salvageable before we start construction. But we'll toss out all the food. I don't want to take the chance of anyone getting sick from smoke-damaged or expired food."

"And I better go upstairs to check on my condo. Before we go our separate ways, my hacker got back to me," Po Po said.

Raina almost felt guilty for the sudden flush of anticipation. Maybe this was the last clue to solving Alonso's murder. "Who was the last person to call Alonso?"

"She only gave me the phone number, not the name. So, I called the number, and it went to voicemail."

Raina rolled her hand, hoping to speed her grandma up. "And this person is?"

Po Po gave Raina a satisfied smile. "Valerie Escalante."

18

UPSIDE DOWN

Raina ducked under the crime scene tape and went into the kitchen. Her mind reeled from the information her grandma had dropped moments before. Maybe Valerie had killed Alonso under the misguided assumption that her daughter would inherit the money. Valerie was in the garden outside the building at the time of the fire. Unfortunately, she had killed Alonso before he had the chance to include Flora in the will.

The two scorched refrigerators would have to be replaced. Raina couldn't even open the door of the fridge closest to the stove. The second refrigerator opened to forty degrees. Several bagged salads, a potato salad, a Pyrex container of moldy meat, a fruit bowl, and soggy egg rolls. Nothing salvageable. They would haul the refrigerators to the dump.

Some of the utensils, plates, and bakeware from the

cupboards could be salvaged. What should she do with the can of paint thinner? It had Alex's fingerprints on it. It certainly didn't have anyone's fingerprints from the senior center. Maybe she should keep it as evidence in case Alex reversed her decision.

Raina grabbed a gallon Ziploc bag and flipped it inside out. Putting her hand through the bag, she grabbed the can of paint thinner, flipped the bag, and sealed it inside. She closed the cupboard and jerked back in surprise. How long had Flora Escalante been standing in the entryway?

"Sorry. Did I frighten you?" Flora asked sheepishly.

"What are you doing here?" Raina blurted out. Her heart thumped rapidly in her chest. She didn't mean to sound unwelcoming, but Flora could have said something or made a noise to let Raina know she was in the room.

The redhead blushed with embarrassment. She wore a black T-shirt and dark blue skinny jeans. She was as sleek as a cat and just as cute.

Now that Raina knew Valerie was the culprit behind Alonso's murder, she couldn't help but feel sorry for Flora. Once Raina told Detective Hopper about Valerie's phone call to lure Alonso into the kitchen, Flora would lose her remaining parent.

"Sorry. I didn't mean to sound so rude, but you startled me," Raina said. "Are you here to see me, or are you looking for someone else?"

"I'm...I'm not sure." Flora swallowed. "I was hoping Detective Hopper would be here."

Raina left the Ziploc bag on the damaged countertop and crossed the kitchen to Flora. Upon closer inspection, the redhead was paler than usual. Her dark eye bags and freckles stood out on her oval face.

"Detective Hopper is not here," Raina said in a soft voice. "Can I help you with something? Do you need a friendly ear?"

"It's my mother," Flora said in a trembling voice.

Raina's eyes widened. Did Flora find out that her mother was her adopted father's murderer? What if she had evidence? "What about your mother?"

Instead of answering Raina, Flora pulled the note from her back pocket and held it out. "Read this, please."

Raina unfolded the paper and read out loud. "I have your mother. Tell no one. Come to the mansion at seven o'clock tonight." She blinked and read the note again to herself. "I don't understand. Did someone kidnap your mother?"

Flora's eyes filled with tears, and she blinked rapidly. She swallowed, and when she replied, her voice wavered. "It's Alonso's murderer. He's out to get our entire family. First, my dad, then Gabriel, and now my mom."

Raina studied the note again. The paper was the same thick linen paper that matched the threatening letter she had received. An inkjet printer printed the kidnapping message. There was no doubt the sender of both notes was the same person. Which should have been Valerie Escalante. If she was the killer, how could she have been kidnapped? Or was this a trick?

"Rainy! Where are you, girl?" Po Po called out from the foyer.

"In the kitchen, Po Po," Raina yelled back.

Po Po hurried into the kitchen, stopping dead in her tracks when she saw Flora. "Rainy, I need to talk to you. It's important."

Raina glanced at Flora. She didn't want to leave the redhead alone. "Do you mind if I tell my grandma about this?" She waved the note in the air.

Flora shook her head. "I need all the help I can get."

Raina handed the note to Po Po. "It's a kidnapping note." As her grandma read the letter, Raina turned to Flora. "Has the kidnapper called about a ransom?"

Flora shook her head. "I went to the police station and spoke to Officer Sokol. He dismissed the note. Said it was a prank."

"This explains why you're looking for Officer Hopper," Raina said.

"I've seen her here with you. I thought maybe the two of you were friends. I was hoping to find her here," Flora said in a rush. She closed her eyes and winced. "Sorry. I'm babbling. I get like this when I am anxious."

"Why did Officer Sokol think the note was a prank?" Raina asked.

"I don't know," Flora said. "He was already in a foul mood when I got there. He took down the police report and said the police would look into it, but that it's likely a prank."

Raina's heart sank. He was probably upset that his stunt with the insurance claim not only didn't work but might backfire on him.

"It's no joke," Po Po said. "Linda William is right. Alonso's murderer is killing off everyone who inherits the money." She pulled a note from her purse and handed it to Raina. "Someone slipped this under my condo's door."

Raina could tell at a glance that her grandma's note came from the same stock as the threatening and kidnapping notes. Geez, this killer had a lot of time to write all these notes. She flipped it open and read out loud. "I have Janice Tally. Tell no one. Come to the mansion at eight o'clock tonight."

A chill ran down Raina's spine. It was like history repeating itself all over again. She wasn't able to save Janice's grandson, but there was still time to save Janice.

Flora gasped, and her hand flew to her mouth. "Isn't Janice my dad's girlfriend?"

Raina nodded reluctantly. She read the letter again. Did the killer think he could dispose of Flora at seven and Po Po at eight?

"What proof do we have that Valerie and Janice are in his hands?" Po Po asked.

"I've been calling my mom for the last few days," Flora said. "I even stopped by her house. I haven't been able to get in touch with her. If Mom is out of town, she would have told me."

"No one has seen or heard from Janice for a few days, too," Raina said.

"What if this is a trap to lure us to the mansion?" Po Po asked. She cut her eyes to Flora. "No offense, but you're a suspect. How do we know you aren't setting us up?"

Flora burst into tears. "I want my mom back. I don't understand why a mad man targeted our family."

Raina gave Flora a sideways glance. The redhead seemed genuinely upset. But if the murderer wasn't Valerie or Flora, then who was this person? Was it Manny? Had the Posse Club taken the killer into their bosom?

Po Po handed Flora a packet of tissues and patted Flora's shoulder. "We need to think this through. We can't go running into a trap."

Flora pleaded with her eyes. "Raina, please help me. We're talking about my mom. And your friend too."

"I'm not sure what you think I can do," Raina said.

"You could hide behind a tree or something. When you jump out, you might scare the killer off. It will be two against one."

Raina gestured at her body. "I'm the size of a pygmy goat. I don't think the killer will be afraid of me."

Tears continued to flow down Flora's face. "What should I do? I can't go by myself."

"Let me call Detective Hopper," Raina said, pulling out her cell phone.

"And if this turns out to be a real kidnapping, then Sokol is dead in the water," Po Po said. "The department will have to get rid of him after this."

Flora blew her nose and glanced at her smartwatch. "I'm running out of time." She straightened. "I better get going. If I get there early, I can search the mansion. Maybe the killer hid my mom there."

Raina pulled up Detective Hopper's number on her phone. "Just one minute. Let me call Joanna."

Flora spun on her heels and ran out of the kitchen.

Raina followed her into the foyer. "Wait, Flora! If it's a trap, you could die."

"I have to save my mom. I have no choice," Flora called out over her shoulder. She ran out of the senior center and disappeared.

"I'm going after her," Raina said.

"No. No, Rainy. It's a trap," Po Po said.

"Maybe. Or maybe not. I don't care about Valerie, but I have to get Janice out. I can't fail her again," Raina said. The two of them had found Janice's grandson's body years ago when they broke into his apartment.

"Then I'm coming with you."

"Not until after you get me some backup. I'm counting on you to save my bacon, Po Po. Call Joanna Hopper's cell phone and her landline. Then call the police station. Hopefully, as Matthew's grandma-in-law, his coworkers will take you seriously."

Po Po nodded. "After I make these calls, then I'll leave for the mansion?"

Raina shook her head. "One more thing. I need you to go upstairs and knock on Manny Díaz's door. If he's at home, then he's not our killer."

"And Flora and Valerie are our killers." Po Po shook her head. "I don't like this."

Raina sighed. "I don't either, but we don't have a choice." She hugged her grandma. "Please hurry."

19

A RESCUE MISSION

Raina parked in the shadow of the trees across from the mansion. If she pulled into the circular driveway, she might alert the killer of her presence. Much safer to hike in and hide among the trees until she got to the building.

The deepening purple sky cast shadows on the sidewalks. Honest folks were home eating dinner. But with the homes spaced far apart, it would take the boom of a grenade launcher to get the neighbors' attention.

Raina hoped help was on the way. She pulled out the pepper spray and Taser and tucked them into her shorts pockets. She closed the car door quietly and jogged across the street. She slipped through the opening of the driveway and trotted toward the house, keeping close to the shadow of the towering trees.

As Raina approached the two-story hacienda, she

slowed her pace. She felt like a woman from a Gothic novel who went off to meet the killer by herself in the middle of the night. The only thing missing was the flowing nightgown and the heaving bosom.

The mansion's exterior lights were on, but the interior was dark. There was no car parked on the circular driveway. Did Flora park in the garage? The overpowering scent of flowers did little to improve Raina's mood. Her eyes became grainy and itchy.

Raina stayed on the edge of the tree canopy and watched the arch windows, waiting for a curtain to flicker. During the drive, Raina had realized that Flora and Valerie were probably working together. If Flora had wanted help, she wouldn't have run off when Raina mentioned calling Detective Hopper.

It would be stupid to come in through the front door or the garage. There had to be another way in through the back door. Raina crept around the side of the mansion. The walkway wrapped around the entire building, and was filled with large potted plants or wood benches every twenty feet. Raina scurried from pot to pot and peered in at the arch windows. The rooms were empty.

After fifteen minutes, she leaned against a pot to catch her breath. The butterflies in her stomach slammed against each other. Where was her backup? If they were coming, they should be here by now. She smacked her forehead with her palm. What if Detective Hopper had to get a warrant? And if this were the case, her grandma wouldn't wait for the police. Should Raina turn back around to intercept her grandma?

Raina glanced at the long row of windows in front of her. Why wasn't there a back door? Who built a house this size without another entrance? It would take too long to look through every window on the first floor. And she didn't have the skills to scale the wall to get to the second floor. She needed a new plan—one where the villains came to her.

She turned and crept back to the garage and used Linda's key to open the side door that led into the garage where she could go through to the house. She stepped inside quickly and closed the door behind her, leaving it unlocked. Her backup might need to sneak in like she did. The butterflies morphed into a concrete block in her stomach. She took several deep breaths to get her bearings and waited for her eyes to adjust to the pitch black.

The tiny windows across the top of the garage doors offered the only illumination in the space. Raina didn't dare turn on her cell phone light. Since she didn't see any cars parked in the circular driveway, Flora and Valerie might have parked their cars in here.

The last time Raina was in this garage, Alonso's white Toyota Camry was in the rear left corner, and the door to the kitchen was on the rear right corner. She strained her eyes but couldn't make out anything this deep inside the tandem garage. She said a small prayer to her ancestors and inched forward with her hands held out in front of her.

After several steps, her foot rammed against something hard. Raina yelped and bent down to rub her toes. The overhead fluorescent lights turned on, and Raina was momentarily blinded. She hunched down even lower, pressing her back against a black car. A bead of sweat rolled down Raina's back. She closed her eyes and prayed.

A few heartbeats later, Raina opened her eyes again. The garage was dark again. One of the Escalante women must have heard a sound in the garage and came to check it out. What if they had seen Raina and were on the other side of the door, waiting for her?

Raina needed a distraction. Something that would divert attention away from the door connecting the kitchen and garage. She pulled out her cell phone and tapped the screen. The faint light showed a clear path between the black car and the connecting door. She trotted the short distance. Pulling out the pepper spray, she called the house and cracked open the connecting door. The coast was clear.

She slipped inside and closed the door gently behind her. The lights from the appliances gave the kitchen a faint glow, just enough to make out the shape of the furnishings.

As Raina crab-walked from the door to the kitchen island, a woman approached from the entryway.

Raina's heart sank. Busted! She held up the pepper

spray with shaking hands. If she kept talking, eventually, the police would get here. A bead of sweat ran down the small of her back. "Where is Janice?"

The woman flicked on the kitchen light and rested her hands on her hips. "What are you doing here?"

Raina blinked at the sudden brightness.

Valerie's Botox face registered no expression, but her eyes glittered with annoyance. Her Betty Boop cleavage was tussled into a tight tank top. Her pencil skirt and heels weren't exactly an outfit made for someone with murder in mind. "And where is my daughter?"

Raina licked her lips nervously. Was Valerie toying with her? "I thought you were kidnapped."

"Don't be ridiculous," Valerie said. She glanced around the kitchen and pressed her lips into a thin line. "Is she upstairs?"

Now Raina was confused. If Valerie was in cahoots with Flora, wouldn't she know where her daughter stashed Janice? "Did you call Alonso before the fire at the senior center?"

"Yes, but the line was busy. It went straight to voicemail. Now, where is my daughter?" Valerie asked.

Flora appeared behind her mother. "I'm right here."

As Valerie turned, she said, "It's about time—"

Flora whacked Valerie on the head with a candlestick holder. Valerie crumbled to the ground as if somebody had cut off her puppet strings. Her legs were bent at an awkward angle, and blood pumped out from the darkening bruise on the side of her face.

Raina froze. She was too shocked even to breathe.

Flora glanced up from her mother's still form and met Raina's eyes. One corner of her mouth was turned up like she was pleased with herself.

A chill went down Raina's spine. Her breath came out in jagged puffs. "Why?" she said through the numb lips.

"It was all her fault that I didn't have a father figure in my life. The stepfathers and boyfriends came and went like a revolving door. Some of them were good, but most had groping hands. It's no wonder I ended up with an abusive husband."

"But why kill Alonso? Wasn't he one of the good ones? He adopted you."

Flora stepped into the room. "He abandoned me and left me to her—this selfish witch."

Raina edged around the kitchen island, keeping it between the two of them. "He thought you would be better off with your biological mother. He paid child support all these years. None of this was his fault."

"All of it was his fault," Flora screamed. "He should have forgiven her. He should have fought for custody. But he did none of this."

Raina took a step back from the anger in Flora's voice. Even though there was the kitchen island between the two of them, she was afraid that Flora might launch herself across it. "You're right. He wasn't a good guy. He deceived all of us," she said placatingly.

Flora's grip tightened on the bloody candlestick. "And I can't believe the old fool left all the money to you. A nobody."

"Not to me. To the senior center. I'm a temporary co-trustee until I leave this job."

Flora blinked. She stopped for a moment and smiled. "Maybe I can apply for the vacant position once you're dead."

20

DUCT TAPE AND COCONUT BRA

"The police will be here any minute," Raina said in a show of bravado. She winced internally at the quiver in her voice.

"I don't think so. They need a warrant to get into the house. Plenty of time for me to kill you and stage it, so my mother takes the blame for everything."

"They won't believe you. You filed a police report about Valerie's kidnapping."

Flora raised an eyebrow. "Did I?"

"Where's Janice?"

Flora shrugged. "How would I know? I heard you were looking for her when I was at the Venus Café."

Raina's eyes widened. This was the first time the rumor mill worked against her. Everything fell into place. "You took the brisket to the senior center. That's why Alonso stayed in the kitchen. When Valerie called, he was on the phone with you."

Flora laughed. "The idiot was trying to warm it up in the microwave. I hit him with your rolling pin, started the fire, and shoved the container back in your fridge. I didn't think anyone would notice with all the food in there."

Raina shivered at the grating sound.

Flora launched her body at Raina, sliding across the granite kitchen island like she was on the slip and slide.

Raina dodged but wasn't fast enough. Flora hit Raina's shoulder and knocked the pepper spray out of her hands.

They crashed onto the floor in a tangle of arms and legs. Raina got the wind knocked out of her.

Flora rolled and straddled Raina's legs. She held up the candlestick.

Bang!

A gust of wind drifted into the kitchen.

"Raina!" screamed Po Po from the front of the house.

Flora jerked her head in the direction of the sound. She hesitated.

Raina pulled the Taser out of her pocket. Powered it on. A crackle filled the air.

Flora swiveled her glance to Raina, swinging the candlestick.

Raina blocked it with one hand. Pain ran up her forearm. She jammed the Taser into Flora's neck.

The killer crumbled to the floor, twitching.

Po Po ran into the kitchen with a baseball bat. Her gaze shifted from Raina to Flora. "We better tie her up. Detective Hopper has to get a warrant. It might be a while before the police get here."

While Po Po pulled out a roll of duct tape from her beach bag-sized purse, Raina got up from the floor. Why her grandma had duct tape with her was a question for another time. Po Po wrapped the duct tape around Flora's hands.

Raina's cell phone chirped with an incoming message. She pulled it out and tapped on the app. The message was from Janice.

AT GRANDDAUGHTER'S APARTMENT. DON'T WORRY ABOUT ME.

She put the phone away and sighed. "Janice is with her granddaughter."

"I always hate it when victims don't appreciate getting rescued," Po Po said.

"Or that heroes are labeled as busybodies," Raina said.

They laughed until tears rolled down their faces, and the tension melted from Raina's shoulders. Po Po went to check on Valerie, and Raina called nine-one-one for an ambulance.

THREE MONTHS LATER, Raina hit the button on her playlist to set the mood for the luau dinner at the senior center. With the money from the trust fund, she had paid the Venus Café to cater the meal. Large chafing dishes for the buffet lined the new granite countertops in the kitchen.

Her grandma had dimmed the lights and turned on the box to project moving pineapples on the opposite wall. Who knew she could change the image from her remote?

Tables were set out in the recreation room for the friends and family that would come for the reopening. As folks drifted in, Raina felt a sense of satisfaction settling in her chest.

Detective Hopper joined Raina at the dessert table inside the recreation room. "Looks like another bang-up job for our local amateur sleuth."

Raina stiffened. She wouldn't let anyone burst her bubble today. "You sound bitter."

Detective Hopper picked up a piece of brownie and set it on her plate. "You helped me crack my first case as lead detective. Trust me. There is no bitterness here."

"Uh-huh."

"I had to say those harsh words the last time we spoke because I feared for your safety. The trust fund set you up to be the next victim. I had to tell you to butt out for your own good."

Raina tidied up the napkins at the end of the table.

She didn't believe the policewoman for one minute. "Is that right?"

"Well, I'm glad we're still friends," Detective Hopper said, oblivious. "Flora confessed to both murders."

"Why did she kill Gabriel?"

"Flora thought she would be the contingent beneficiary."

"So, in the end, it was about the money after all."

"It's what makes the world go around." Detective Hopper drifted off with the brownie in her mouth.

Raina took a deep breath and glanced around the room. Her grandma held court at a table with members of the Posse Club. She was in a coconut bra and a grass skirt with a flower lei. Her grandma was probably regaling them on her latest investigation —again.

Janice Tally came into the recreation room, pushing her walker in front of her. Like most of the folks at the dinner, she wore a Hawaiian shirt.

The retiree had gone into hiding at her granddaughter's apartment after the confrontation with Valerie. It took a visit from the police to convince her to come home after Flora's arrest. She glanced at Po Po, and her lips tightened into a thin line. She spotted Raina and waved for her to come over.

Raina strode over with a sinking heart. Within weeks, Janice and her grandma were back to their usual bickering selves. "Hi, Janice. Do you need anything?"

Janice reached into the fabric pocket dangling in front of her walker and pulled out an envelope. "This is for you, my dear."

Raina opened the envelope and glanced inside. She gasped. "I can't take this."

"Sure, you can. You never went on a honeymoon with your handsome husband."

Raina tried to put the envelope back into the walker's pocket. "It's too much money."

Janice batted at Raina's hand. "After what you've gone through for us, for me, you deserve it. And it's not really my money. It's from the money that Alonso gave me."

"Then save it for yourself."

Po Po saddled up next to Janice, holding two flower leis in their hands. She draped one over Raina's head and dropped the other on Janice's walker. Probably so the two wouldn't appear too friendly in front of the other people in the room.

Up close, Raina saw that her grandma wore a beige tank top underneath the coconut bra. She sighed inwardly. At least she wouldn't get complaints about indecency later.

"What's going on here? Are you bullying my granddaughter now?" Po Po asked.

"I gave her the tickets," Janice said.

Po Po broke into a wide smile. "Take it, Rainy. Who

knows when you'll get another opportunity to spend her money." She jerked her thumb at Janice.

"You knew about this," Raina said, shaking the envelope at her grandma.

Po Po folded her arms around her chest. "I might have given her some ideas."

Janice rolled her eyes. "She refused to let me buy tickets anywhere else. Your grandma is a big bully."

The three of them laughed out loud.

THE END

Anne is hard at work at the next book. If you want a new release alert, sign up here: https://www. subscribepage.com/RainaSun

Meet Lucy Fong
Just Shoot Me Dead
(Lucy Fong Mystery #1)

ACKNOWLEDGMENTS

A story is a dream that a writer brings to life on paper. But a book needs a team to nurture it into the enjoyable tale you've just read.

I want to thank my editors, Alicia S. and Brandee, for wrangling my words so they are coherent.

And then, there are my wonderful beta-readers—Joyce S., Cindy I., Della D., Susan J., and Debi P.—thank you, ladies, for volunteering your time to catch these sneaky typos and grammatical errors.

And finally, thank you, Susan C. for the awesome cover.

I wouldn't have been able to bring this story to life without all of you, wonderful ladies. Thank you!

—Anne R. Tan

ALSO BY ANNE R. TAN

Thanks for reading *Fair Cronies and Felonies*. I hope you enjoyed it!

Want to know about new releases, sale pricing, and exclusive content?

Sign up for Anne R. Tan's Readers Club newsletter at http://annertan.com/newsletter

Your information would not be sold or transferred. Thank you for trusting me with your email.

Want More Raina Sun?

Raining Men and Corpses (Raina Sun #1)

Gusty Lovers and Cadavers (Raina Sun #2)

Breezy Friends and Bodies (Raina Sun #3)

Balmy Darlings and Death (Raina Sun #4)

Sunny Mates and Murders (Raina Sun #5)

Murky Passions and Scandals (Raina Sun #6)

Smoldering Flames and Secrets (Raina Sun #7)

Hazy Grooms and Homicides (Raina Sun #8)

Chilly Comforts and Disasters (Raina Sun #9)

Fair Cronies and Felonies (Raina Sun #10)

How about another series by Anne R. Tan?

Just Shoot Me Dead (Lucy Fong #1)

Just Lost and Found (Lucy Fong #1.5)

Just a Lucy Break-In (Lucy Fong #2)

JUST SHOOT ME DEAD

As the trill of the seldom-used ring tone filled the air, Lucy Fong jerked in her seat like someone had stabbed her rear with a needle, and the dumpling squirted out of her chopsticks, smacking into her date's glasses. It slid down his shirt before disappearing under the table, leaving a trail of grease and disappointment in its wake. She closed her eyes, wishing for a wormhole to open up beneath her feet.

In the last sixteen years, her estranged mother had only called her once, and that was when Lucy's stepfather had died. What bad news heralded the call this time? If it were good news, her half-sister would have posted it on social media by now. The conversation in the Chinese restaurant didn't miss a beat, and the clatter of eating utensils scraped against plates continued unabashed. Lucy's world had tilted on its axis, and no one had noticed.

Lucy opened her eyes, smiling like Miss America on steroids. "Sorry. At least it wasn't red wine." She was supposed to have dinner with just her grandma this evening but had accepted the extra dinner companions —a nice Chinese doctor and his mama—with grace. This wasn't the first set-up, but it would be the last. Her cell phone vibrated to indicate Mom had left a voicemail.

"I've gotten a drink thrown in my face, but never a dumpling." The doctor wiped his glasses, smearing the grease across the lens. "I'm always up for new experiences."

Lucy's smile wobbled. Ah, a man with a sense of humor. A rare commodity these days. Too bad this was like everything else in her life—the timing was off. She was still working with her therapist to fix the clock. "It must be rewarding to save people every day."

"I don't help people because it's rewarding. I help people because it's the right thing to do," the doctor said, sounding like he believed every word.

Lucy groaned inwardly. A do-gooder. He was definitely too good for the likes of her. She wasn't a "bad girl" by any stretch, but she certainly wasn't an ideal wife for a Chinese doctor from a long line of Chinese doctors. She snorted. She pitied the poor woman who did meet those ideals.

The doctor's mama scowled at Lucy. She probably wanted a nice Chinese girl for her precious boy and got a half-Chinese girl instead. The woman had insisted on speaking in Cantonese during the entire meal and giving Po Po pointed looks whenever Lucy stumbled over the words with her thick American accent. "I guess you're not much use in the kitchen if you can't even handle chopsticks."

"Lucy is an internet whizbang. Maybe she could help advertise your son's business?" Po Po said.

The doctor's mama stiffened. "That wouldn't be necessary."

Lucy wanted to slap money on the table for the meal and walk out the door. She didn't need this after a full week of work. But her grandma was all the family she had left...or all the family she wanted in her life. She glanced at Po Po, and the hopeful look on her grandma's face fizzled out.

Po Po filled the awkward silence with chatter about a murder investigation. Her grandma had recently cut off her long silver braid to favor a short pixie cut with pink streaks much like Lucy's. When Po Po got to the car chase in her story, Lucy tuned her out. Her grandma read too many mystery books as far as Lucy was concerned. The matriarch of the Wong family should have been Irish for all the gab she spun.

Lucy snorted, earning another dark look from the doctor's mama. Speaking of mothers, she better see what Mom wanted.

"Sorry, I need to take this call. It's from my mother," Lucy said, pushing back her chair.

Po Po's eyes widened with concern, and she bit her

lower lip as if to stop herself from saying something. She knew all about Lucy's tenuous relationship with her mother and half-sister.

"It's fine. We're done here," the doctor's mom said, dabbing at her lips with the cloth napkin.

Lucy thanked the doctor for a lovely dinner and shifted her gaze to Po Po. "I'll wait for you outside." She stumbled out of the restaurant, her heart pounding at the rejection from the doctor's family and the bruise to her ego.

The fog snaked around the red lanterns hung on the streets for the Chinatown tourists. Lucy shivered, but not from the chilly November night. Her hands shook when she pulled her cell phone from her purse. She tapped on the screen to listen to the voicemail, but instead of Mom's voice, the caller identified herself as Cousin Estelle.

Your mother is in the hospital. A neighbor found her shot in the stomach at her private investigation office. Lucy dear, you need to come home.

Her hands became numb, and the cell phone slipped onto the sidewalk. This couldn't be happening...

From behind her, she heard Po Po say goodnight to their dinner companions. Lucy swallowed the urge to throw up. Hurling the dumplings on the sidewalk would kill her reputation. The doctor's mama would make sure everyone knew Po Po's granddaughter was either a drunk or drug addict. San Francisco might be a big city, but Chinatown was a small community.

"Are you okay? What did your mother want?" Po Po said, rubbing Lucy's hunched back.

"It was her cousin. Mom is in the hospital," Lucy whispered, swallowing at the catch in her voice.

Po Po's lined face closed in like a flower petal. "Let's get you home, so you can pack to leave in the morning." She scooped up the cell phone and its battery off the sidewalk. "Broken. Why am I not surprised?" She tucked the phone into her purse. "Lucky you. I have a spare prepaid phone."

They strolled toward the brick three-story building two blocks away. The first floor housed the Fong Chinese Herbal Shop that once belonged to Lucy's deceased uncle. His apprentice ran the shop for her now. They got into the elevator, and Po Po hit the button for the third floor.

The keys rattled in Lucy's hand, and it took her three tries before she could open the door to her small apartment. She had lost a bedroom in the elevator renovation for the building, but it had been worth it. Her uncle had stayed in his home in the apartment across the hall until the end six months ago.

Once inside her small apartment, Po Po bustled around making tea in the plain terra cotta set her uncle had given her. The little ritual seemed out of place, given the gravity of the news, but comforting at the same time. Her uncle had done the same ritual when Lucy had shown up on his doorstep as a teenager in the middle of the night.

She glanced at the lucky cat clock on the wall with its plastic swaying tail. Eight thirty. If she left now, she might make it to the hospital by one in the morning. She glanced out the window. The thick fog hid the building next door, except for one speck of glow that might have been a window. Maybe it would be closer to two in the morning by the time she rolled into Morro Cliff Village, a small coastal hamlet on the Central Coast.

It would make more sense to leave in the morning and be much safer for a woman traveling alone. But what if Mom didn't make it through the night? Though they no longer had a close mother-daughter relationship, they once did. She blinked at the tears burning in the back of her eyes. She was going to be too late...

Po Po wrapped Lucy's hands around a steaming cup of tea. "It's only too late when you give up. We can swing by my house on the way out of the City. I can pack a bag in less than ten minutes."

When Lucy's late uncle had taken her in, this generous woman had claimed Lucy as one of her own, welcoming the angry teen into the Wong family all those years ago. She would do anything for this woman, but this wasn't the kind of road trip for Po Po to tag along.

"I want to go alone. I need the time to think," Lucy said.

"You can't drive like this. You're still in shock," Po Po said.

Lucy shook her head. "I'm fine. It's just...I thought there would be more time."

The fluorescent lights flickered overhead, casting a sick gray pallor over the hospital room despite the cheerful yellow walls. The lights were dim, and the room was only big enough to hold the hospital bed and chair. On the wall opposite the entrance was a tall and narrow window like the kind found in a medieval castle and a door that led to the bathroom. The only sounds in the room were the beeping and whirring machines that kept Mom alive.

Lucy stood with her hands tucked under her armpits at the footboard of the hospital bed, mesmerized by her mother's still form. She didn't recognize the woman in front of her. The mother in Lucy's memory was a tall and willowy woman with thick blonde hair. Lucy had inherited her Chinese father's black hair and the Fong family's love for pastries. She considered it a small miracle she still had the metabolism of her youth.

Mom had teased Lucy for being such a serious and reserved child. Whereas, Mom had been a vibrant woman, expressive and passionate, using her entire body when she moved or spoke. Or at least she did years ago. The elderly woman in front of Lucy had a permanent frown in her rail yard of a face. Her body was more shrunken than lush, and the blonde had become a mane of white. The years since her stepfather's death had been hard on Mom, and it showed.

Lucy willed herself to feel something, but there was nothing. The long drive in the dark had shuffled the fear into a corner. There was no sadness, no pain. Sure, Mom had chosen her husband and half-sister over Lucy, but that was a long time ago. Water under the bridge according to her therapist. And the anger had disappeared when her stepfather had died.

She just felt tired...and numb. Before the clumsy blind date, it had been a long day in the office, and her manager had screamed at Lucy for a data entry typo from a co-worker who was still on probation. Granted, as an internet marketing consultant, a single digit on a spreadsheet could kill an ad campaign, but it wasn't a gunshot wound.

Cousin Estelle slept awkwardly on the chair in the corner, her head leaning against the wall. She was actually her mom's younger cousin and in her mid-fifties. She had been a slender woman with too big front teeth and large ears when Lucy had left town. She had also been the unlucky recipient to inherit Great-grandma's first name. While she couldn't do anything with her teeth, her long dyed blonde hair hid the ears. Unfortunately, she had also grown in girth to match them.

Estelle jerked in her sleep and caught herself in time to keep from falling off the chair. She rubbed her sleepy hazel eyes and blinked at Lucy. She paused as if movement might make Lucy disappear.

"Thanks for calling me," Lucy whispered.

Estelle leapt off the chair and swept Lucy into a hug. Like the rest of the women in the Faye's side of the family, Estelle towered over Lucy at close to six feet tall. "It's so good to see you again." She pulled away, studying Lucy from head to toe. "Wow, you've grown into a little cutie pie."

Lucy raised an eyebrow. Little? In Chinatown, she had been as tall as most of the Chinese men at five foot six. She shook the random thoughts from her head. She wasn't here for a homecoming. "What happened?"

"I told you everything I know. You might want to talk to Max DeWitt later this morning. He's the town police chief now," Estelle said.

Lucy blinked. The last name DeWitt sounded familiar, and obviously, Estelle believed Lucy should remember him. "Did you talk to the doctor?"

Estelle shook her head. "Max tracked me down after your mom came out of surgery. The doctor makes his rounds in the morning around nine or ten. The nurse said your mother's condition is stable."

Lucy exhaled in relief. Stable sounded good. Maybe Mom would be back on her feet in a day or two, and Lucy could go home. "I can stay here if you want to go home."

Estelle held out a set of keys. "Why don't you go home and get some sleep? You have a long day ahead of you. I can't find your sister, and there wasn't anyone else…" She took a deep breath. "Do you want me to call a cleaning service for the office?" The words tumbled out in a nervous rush.

Lucy stiffened, trying to stop the shiver down her spine at the mention of the private investigation office. How much blood… She slammed a lid on the thought. "I'll deal with it later. Let me give you the number to my prepaid phone. It's a temporary loaner." She dug in her purse and came up with a receipt. She wrote down the number for her grandma's spare cell phone.

Estelle tucked the slip of paper into her bag. "After you settle in, maybe we can have dinner or…"

Lucy grabbed the spare keys and stumbled toward the door. Settle in? She wasn't staying. "Thank you for everything," she said over her shoulder. She couldn't stand another minute of the whirling machines.

In her haste, Lucy didn't see the man on the other side of the threshold. She stepped on his toe, and her head rammed into his chest. She would have fallen if he hadn't grabbed onto her forearms.

When Lucy straightened, she suppressed a sigh. Could this day get any worse?

"Max," Estelle said. Her voice brightened at his

appearance. "This is Lucy Fong, Dahlia Faye's...uh...daughter."

Lucy ground her teeth. Estelle was about to say bastard daughter. She couldn't believe people still remembered—or cared—that she was born out of wedlock. She shouldn't have come back. There wasn't anything she could do for her mother. She would only get insulted and shunned as she did in her childhood for being different. For having black hair among those with blonde or brown hair. For having slightly slanted eyes—

"Miss Fong, can I get you some coffee or tea?" Max DeWitt asked, his face concerned. "You seem to be in shock."

Lucy shook off his hands. "I'm fine. I need to go." Edging around Estelle and Max, she backed out of the room. Neither of them moved to stop Lucy, but she ran like the past might catch up with her.

The drive to Mom's three-bedroom Cape Cod house was a blur. One moment, Lucy was backing out of the parking spot of the hospital, and the next she was on the gravel path in front of the house, breathing in the salt air. She couldn't remember if she blew through stop signs or sped through the small waterfront downtown area. It was a good thing the shops weren't open for business yet.

When Lucy opened the front door to let herself in, her hands shook and jiggled the keys. It had to be from hunger. She refused to believe a woman she hadn't seen for over a decade would have this kind of impact on her. After all, the phone call from Estelle had interrupted dinner. After she checked in the attic bedroom, she would fish out the granola bar in her purse.

As she made her way up the stairs, Lucy caught glimpses of the ocean through the windows. The pale moonlight sparkled over the dark water. Though the ocean was tranquil from this angle, she knew it crashed against the rocks below the cliff.

Her steps thudded loudly in the silent house. For a moment, as the door to her old attic bedroom swung open, Lucy held her breath as if waiting for her half-sister to pop out from the closet. Of course, there was no chubby-cheeked preschooler. It had been sixteen years.

The room was just as she had left it—a twin bed against one wall, a desk next to a dormer window, and a small trunk against the far wall. The baseball bat was probably still underneath the bed. The posters of her teen idols curled on the edges, and the tape yellowed with age. Mom hadn't even cared enough to come up here to dust.

Continue Lucy's story.
Just Shoot Me Dead

ABOUT THE AUTHOR

Anne R. Tan is a *USA Today* bestselling author. She writes the Raina Sun Mystery series and the Lucy Fong Mystery series. Her humorous cozy mysteries feature Chinese-American amateur sleuths dealing with love, family, and life while solving murders.

Sign up for her newsletter for new release announcement, sales, and exclusive content at http://annertan.com/newsletter/

www.ingramcontent.com/pod-product-compliance
Lightning Source LLC
Chambersburg PA
CBHW021135190726
48288CB00008B/2675